THE DRAGON PRINCE'S LIBRARIAN

ELVA BIRCH

Copyright © 2020 by Elva Birch

All rights reserved.

ROYAL DRAGONS OF ALASKA

This book is part of the Royal Dragons of Alaska series. All of my work stands alone (always a satisfying happy ever after and no cliffhangers!) but there is a story arc across books. This is the order the series may be most enjoyed:

> The Dragon Prince of Alaska (Book 1)
> The Dragon Prince's Librarian (Book 2)
> The Dragon Prince's Bride (Book 3)
> The Dragon Prince's Secret (Book 4)
> The Dragon Prince's Magic (Book 5)

Subscribe to Elva Birch's mailing list and join her in her Reader's Retreat at Facebook for sneak previews and news!

PROLOGUE

*H*is first email was short, and completely professional.

To: t.perez@floridaulibrary.edu
From: northernbookwyrm@alaska.sk
Subj: Thesis topic
For the attention of Ms. Tania Perez,

I received your contact information from the University of Florida, Orlando, and have several questions regarding the topic of your thesis regarding the Small Kingdoms Compact and its symbolic shift. Please contact me at your convenience. I am including my direct phone number if you would prefer that method of correspondence.

Thank you for your time,
Rian

Rian, Tania noted. A pretentious mis-spelling of a common name, or a classical Irish name? She was going to guess pretentious.

Her first email was curt, and she could not quite keep her bitterness from it.

To: northernbookwyrm@alaska.sk
From: t.perez@floridaulibrary.edu
Subj: Re: Thesis topic

*A correspondence: A **written** or **digital** communication exchanged by two parties. I would prefer to continue any contact via email and do not share my direct phone number.*

Also, you should be advised that the thesis is not currently in progress and I no longer have a copy of it, nor of the source material.

I am only a circulation librarian; you would be better served by contacting a Compact scholar with active research work.

Sincerelui,
Tania Perez

She didn't offer to point him towards such a scholar, deleted his email as soon as she replied, and expected to hear nothing more.

To her surprise, he replied with a graphic in Tolkien's Elvish that translated to *gratitude*. It would have been more sensible to assume her valediction was French than Elvish and Tania felt her ire thaw a bit even before she read the rest.

The email continued:

I appreciate your reply and your candor. I have a particular interest in your theories regarding mates and diplomatic bonds and have also seen the same obscure version of the Compact that you originally referenced.

Tania actually closed the email at that point, stood up, and shelved books until she could bear to return to the circulation desk to read the rest of the message.

It had been almost a year since her thesis had vanished.

It wasn't just a single missing file or a random computer error. The hard copies she had printed were stolen out of her apartment while she was out, along with her copy of the old Compact, and her notes. There was no sign of a break-in—her front door was still locked! It was just seamlessly, completely, all gone. She hadn't even been able to call the police, because she had no idea how to explain that only very specific, *valueless* paperwork had gone missing, and files on a computer with a lock code had been carefully deleted.

It was like ninjas had taken it.

She'd gone to her advisor, and gotten very cagey answers about a crashed computer; for some reason, none of the drafts that she'd sent him could be found, in email or in his personal files. He claimed he would search for the hardcopy drafts, then simply never returned to the University after the holiday break; Tania returned from the hiatus to find his office empty and a flailing graduate student struggling to cover his classes.

Tania went to the dean of the college and quarreled with his secretary, who claimed that Tania didn't even have a prospectus filed with the history department. Her student ID was in the database, but her topic was *undeclared*.

Undeclared.

She'd spent her entire undergraduate career sure of what she was going to write, compiling notes, trying to find an advisor who would be a good match for the paper she wanted to work on. She had worked for nearly a year (going through four advisors) to get her premise and outline approved.

She tried to find anyone who remembered her, or her paper, but found only blank stares and head shakes; she was one student among thousands, another unremarkable face that they barely recalled. A few vaguely remembered the topic she'd been interested in, but not enough particulars to be useful.

She staggered through her classes, but couldn't maintain both the course load and the fight to find a new advisor and declare a new topic, and she couldn't simply redo her original thesis with her primary source document mysteriously missing from the library. No other school or research library seemed to have a copy, or even knew what she was referring to. At the end of the semester, struggling with her health, she was informed that her grades were not sufficient to keep her scholarship, and she still had *undeclared* for her thesis. If she could not pay, she could not continue as a student...and if she could not continue as a student, she was no longer eligible for her part-time library job after the summer break. The library director, not wanting to lose her, offered her full-time work for the fall, when their leniency would expire. With nothing else to do, and a desperate need for the health insurance that came with it, she accepted the job.

It was a surreal year, and Tania spent most of it questioning her own sanity.

But Rian...Rian *believed* her. Rian *knew* about the original Compact. Maybe she *wasn't* crazy.

It was with shaking hands that Tania logged back into her email and read the rest.

He casually mentioned the curious *dragons* reference that had gotten her side-eyed by respectable researchers, and asked about her interpretation of the *mate* language.

Tania put her head in her hands and was not sure if

she laughed or cried, only knew that she was a tumble of crazy emotion.

Then she sat down and wrote back, in great detail, answering his questions and offering her own in return.

It wasn't long before he replied, and they exchanged a flurry of emailed letters, each longer than the last, as they dug into the language that she remembered, and her theories about the stranger points.

It all makes sense, she wrote, *if you keep in mind that the dragons referenced are a metaphor for the royal families. The 'protector of the lands' stuff falls into place. Possibly, the fire is an analogy for a weapon or a defensive force. I mean, I suppose it's possible they actually were dragons at the time of the Old Compact. That would explain a lot! Hahahaha.*

When he did not consider her ideas too outlandish to bear, she even, very hesitantly, with a winking emoji, suggested that the formality of the language had the kind of specificity of a ritual, or a magic spell.

His email in response treated the idea with grave consideration, and he offered a few ideas in return that made Tania long for the copy she'd had. There were so many things she would have liked to go back and double-check.

Their emails devolved into stories about their jobs, about the food they were eating, and most of all, about the books they were reading.

Some days, the letters were the only thing hauling her out of her bed, and she would check for his messages first thing, replying while she ate breakfast and decided how much she could do that day. The red flag announcing new mail became an object of joy, and she found herself lurking at her inbox at every opportunity.

They became the glowing high point of Tania's life...until she feared she was developing an unhealthy crush on someone she didn't even know, and decided to search for Rian's real identity.

The email address was her first clue. She assumed, from the address, and his mention of a uniform, that he was in some kind of security, so she went looking for more about an event he'd disparaged.

I have been to these parties, Rian told her. *It's like they read books to hate them.*

That led her to sites that she didn't usually visit, gossipy royal news sources that specialized in paparazzi photos. She was looking at the staff in the background when one of the captions caught her eye.

Twin brothers Prianriakist and Grantraykist attended the event...

Prianriakist. Prian. *Rian.*

Tania had to chuckle and lean her forehead onto her hand. Rian wasn't a pretentious mis-spelling, it was his *casual* name.

She read back through every email he'd ever sent her, and felt supremely stupid.

Of course he was a prince: the cultured tone of his writing, the oblique references to high-brow parties. His intimate knowledge of the Compact and other legal treaties.

In retrospect, it had been completely obvious.

He was a prince.

And she *wasn't* a princess.

~

To: t.perez@floridaulibrary.edu
From: northernbookwyrm@alaska.sk
Subj: Hello?

Tania,

I don't want to be that guy, but it's been a week since you wrote back, and I'm getting worried. I got the book you recommended, and you're right, he's a blow-hard. I was hoping to get your opinion on the chapter talking about succession.

And...I miss you. I've missed your letters this week, and I don't want to seem like a stalker, but it's not like you not to write back. I hope you're okay.

Yours, Rian

To: t.perez@floridaulibrary.edu
 From: northernbookwyrm@alaska.sk
 Subj: Re: Hello?

Dearest Tania,

Please let me know that you're alright and I haven't made you angry. If I said, or did anything, let me know and tell me how to make it right. I haven't heard from you in ten days, and I'm worried for you.

Yours always,
 Rian

To: northernbookwyrm@alaska.sk
 From: Mailer-daemon@floridaulibrary.edu
 Subj: Mail System Error, Re: Hello?

This message was undeliverable, recipient unknown. Please contact a system administrator if you believe this is in error.

1

This was going to be the greatest 'I told you so' in history, Rian thought. He was sweating in the Florida humidity and reconsidering the uniform that had seemed so sensible in Alaska in October.

"She's not your mate," his twin brother Tray had insisted. "She's a *pen pal*. The Compact already tapped a new queen for Alaska. Why would there be more than one? So that Fask could be king, maybe. You? No."

But Rian knew before Tania opened the door to her apartment that he wasn't here by accident. He hadn't imagined that undeniable pull whenever he thought of her, and his dragon was steaming in his head, absolutely certain and utterly focused.

This is where we need to be, he told Rian firmly. *This is the time.*

And when he saw her at last, she was weirdly familiar and entirely new; Rian couldn't stop himself from staring. She looked like her surreptitious photographs, wavy dark hair with fading blonde highlights framing a round, tawny-skinned face. Brown eyes with layers of gold gazed back under bangs that were too long.

Did she feel the same recognition that he felt? She didn't look particularly welcoming, but it was hard to parse around the flood of emotions and feelings he was simmering in. His? His dragon's? *Hers?* Even his body didn't feel like it was entirely his own, which wasn't entirely *pleasant.*

"What do you want?" she asked, and her voice sent shivers down his spine.

"I tried to call," he explained. "And before that, I emailed."

It had only been emails, at first, starting from one carefully worded query about Tania's thesis—a thesis that had been wiped by Small Kingdoms agents from her university's database almost a year before.

Her first reply, more than a month ago, had been understandably defensive.

The document she had been working from was a secret version of the international treaty called the Compact, and had never been intended for general consumption. The public version had been greatly sterilized, removing all mention of dragons, magic, mates, and casters.

She'd written most of a thesis on the document before Small Kingdoms agents got wind of it, and operatives had moved in decisively, deleting the thesis, her copies, the copies of the secret Compact at the library, and even her prospectus in the university database. Her advisor had been amply paid off to pursue a sudden change of profession.

Once Rian had assured her that she wasn't crazy, that he had *seen* the same Compact she remembered, they traded a flurry of emails on the topic...and later went completely off-topic as they connected through a long string of letters. Rian's life had narrowed to her correspondence; he had never guessed he would meet anyone with her clever turn of phrases who shared his interest in books. Every email was anticipated more eagerly than the last, every red flag on his phone was a reason to shirk his duties and disappear. He read them over and over, composing his replies with care.

And then they stopped coming.

"The library froze my email when I got fired," Tania said coldly. "And my phone is off." Then, suspiciously, "How did you get my number? How did you know where I lived?"

Rian flushed. "I hired an investigator." He swiftly put up his hands. "Not that I was stalking you, but your emails started bouncing, so I called the library, and they wouldn't give me any way to contact you. I was worried for you. I couldn't sleep. I needed to know that you were okay." He ran his fingers through his hair in nervous habit. "I'm not making myself sound any less like a stalker…"

"I'm fine," she said, and in a rush, Rian realized that he knew she was lying. She was barely holding on. She was afraid, and she was in pain. He could feel the ache in her hips and her shoulders, and the exhaustion she was fighting.

"You're not fine," he blurted.

He really did think she was going to shut the door on him then.

"No, I'm sorry," he said swiftly. "You're fine. I mean, and you're definitely *fine*. I just don't mean…" Why couldn't he be suave like Toren or Fask? he wondered desperately. She probably thought he was leering at her, because he couldn't stop staring at her in wonder.

Tania's scowl softened a little. "You're not what I expected from a prince," she said, confirming that she'd long since figured out exactly who he was. It probably hadn't taken her a private investigator.

"I'm not," Rian agreed. "I mean, I'm a prince, but I don't fit much of the prince...expectation. Sorry."

"The uniform helps," she said, with a tiny quirk of a smile. "When you said you wore a uniform as part of your day job, I assumed you were in security." Then she glanced out into the hallway behind him. "No escort? No honor guard? Trumpets with long flags off the bottom?"

"I flew alone," Rian explained. Which wasn't much of an explanation, since she didn't know he was a dragon shifter. Yet. "I mean...ah...can I come in?" He certainly wasn't going to reveal that information in the dark, muggy common hall of her apartment building.

She gave him a deeply considering look and finally stepped aside, a little hitch to her step that Rian *knew* caused her pain.

Her apartment was small, just what Rian could charitably call cozy, and untidy. It was also completely lined in books. There were bookshelves on every free wall, a short shelf behind the couch, high shelves above the cabinets in the kitchen stuffed with cookbooks, even a narrow shelf just two books wide next to the door. Further piles of books were scattered on the coffee and end tables. Above the table, the only clear wall was decorated in old photographs and certificates.

It smelled like old books and vanilla, which seemed absolutely perfect.

"What do you want?" Tania asked again.

Rian thought it sounded less chilly this time, and more weary. He resisted the urge, just barely, to fold her into his arms and promise that everything was going to be okay now.

"I needed to talk to you," he said seriously.

"About the Compact?" Tania asked. "There are other scholars. Scholars of the *real* version, not the fanciful version I might have imagined."

"You didn't imagine it."

She seemed taken aback by his firmness. Rather than clearing him a seat, she sank into the one empty chair like she didn't have anything left for courtesy. Maybe she didn't. Rian took a stack of books with library bands off of the other chair and moved it to the table.

Tell her, his dragon hissed at him. *Tell her everything.*

She waited for him to go on, and Rian took a moment to compose himself and stuff his over-eager dragon back into silence.

"I'm really sorry about your thesis," he started. "It's...kind of my fault that it got scrapped. I mean, not mine personally, but...there are two versions of the Compact. The one you saw...you weren't supposed to see. I mean, I think you *were* supposed to see it, because otherwise I'd never have met you, but it's not for...public consumption."

Tania stared at him in confusion. "How is it your fault that there are two versions? I thought it was just an...older version. Why would there be two current versions? Why are they so different?"

"There are two versions to protect me. To protect my family. To protect our secrets. That stuff you thought was metaphor, about dragons and magic...that's real. We just don't share that copy with other countries because people would look at us...well, yes, exactly like that."

She looked deeply dubious.

"It's literal," Rian explained. "In fact, it's pretty exactingly literal, because it's a really long and involved spell, and you have to be really specific with spells or they can take off in unexpected directions."

Tania laughed. "The royal families of the Small Kingdoms, they are all dragons. And the Compact is a *spell*."

Rian suspected that she was reconsidering her decision to let him into her apartment. "Please, hear me out! Magic is real, there *are* dragons, and I'm not a stalker!"

"So you keep insisting," Tania said, and Rian couldn't help but grin at her, because it was exactly something she would have written in an email.

"Do you believe me?" he asked hopefully.

"I shouldn't," Tania said, frowning at him. "I shouldn't, there is no practical reason that I would, and I don't understand why I do."

Rian smiled. "You will," he said confidently. "You will, so you do."

Tania stared at him. "Supposing this *is* all true, why are you here? What does any of this have to do with me?"

Rian looked at her and chewed over his options. "Do you remember the part of the Compact that talks about mates?"

"'When the need is great and the ground is fertile.' Very poetic stuff." Her eyes narrowed in suspicion. "I presumed it was a way to make an arranged marriage sound more palatable."

"It's a little more than that," Rian said. "When a change of power is needed, the Compact's spell chooses a partner for the heir. It's...not a compulsion exactly, but it makes sure that they meet. And that they know each other when they do."

"Like your brother, Torenayram." Tania was nodding slowly. "I saw the tabloids. Whirlwind romance, love at first sight, all the usual trappings. Was she really a murderer? That seems like a pretty big oversight on the part of a magic piece of paper. Isn't a mate supposed to be a perfect queen?"

"She was framed," Rian said. "The charges were dropped. But yes, Carina is Toren's mate. I have no reason to doubt it." Quite the opposite; now that he was sitting opposite from his own mate, he knew exactly what Toren had gone through.

"I'm still not seeing the relevance to me," Tania said, with an adorable scrunch to her forehead. "Surely there are people with more familiarity with the Compact than me. Even the real version."

"You're *my* mate," Rian finally blurted, and joy rose up in his throat at being able to admit it out loud. *The greatest 'I told you so' in history,* his dragon reminded him smugly.

2

Tania stared at the prince sitting across her cheap kitchen table from her. He gazed at her with a besotted look that she could not reconcile with anything else in her life.

She wasn't sure what to do with anything he'd told her, and she felt like she was having trouble *breathing* around the big, charismatic presence of him.

He was taller than she would have guessed from his photographs—maybe everything in Alaska really was bigger—and in most of the pictures she'd seen, he'd been scowling, like he was irritated with the photographer for interrupting him.

He wasn't scowling now; he was grinning like a drunk loon. His eyes were silvery-gray, and his dark brown hair was just long enough to curl slightly. His haircut probably cost as much as a month of rent. His glasses were light wire frames, giving him just a hint of a studious air. His uniform was deep blue, with eight stars of gold echoing the Alaskan flag arranged at the collar.

Magic.

Magic *would* explain why she desperately wanted to climb into his lap and kiss him.

It was almost like she was feeling too much, like she was being bombarded by emotions that weren't even her own. Elation, affection, anticipation, desire...

When she tried to be analytical, she thought that the attraction she felt made complete sense—he was utterly gorgeous!—but the strongest of the sensations was unexpectedly...safety.

She was safe with Rian, she was utterly, completely *safe*—like she knew him already, and she trusted his impossible words. Was it only because she'd built up such a ridiculous crush on the person behind the emails? She ought to be having serious second thoughts about letting him into her apartment...and somehow, she wasn't. She believed every word he said.

Tania felt her cheeks heat as she remembered some of the less...official photos she'd found online.

He'd lost a bet, and someone had gotten blurry shots of the week he had spent casually naked, drinking coffee and reading books around the castle.

No one online was sure what bet he'd lost.

And now he was *here* claiming that she was his *mate*.

What did you even say to that?

She laughed and shook her head. "Dragons," she said helplessly. "Dragons and magic and *mates*. I thought my life was surreal a few months ago when I thought that maybe ninjas had stolen my thesis."

Rian reached a hand across the table to her. "My mate," he repeated.

Tania looked at his hand, at the long fingers and the perfectly-manicured nails. She hadn't trimmed her own nails in a week or more; it was just one of the many things that didn't seem important at the end of an exhausting day. One of them was broken.

She closed her eyes and for a moment, she could believe without hesitation. She could believe in dragons and magic and all the wonders in her favorite books. She thought it was possible that this was all real, that she was Cinderella about to be whisked away to a castle in a magical carriage—no, on the back of a dragon! True love! Destiny! Rags to riches!

And the prince... She wasn't sure how much of his perfection was because of her silly crush on a guy who could quote Tolkien and write witty emails, and how much of it was that he was this insanely hot guy who looked like he'd dropped out of a grocery store checkout celebrity magazine. He probably was actually *in* those magazines.

She wanted it to be real. She wanted to be the heroine of those books. She wanted to never worry about money again, to never wonder if she should buy groceries or medicine. She wanted...*him.*

She sighed and opened her eyes as her doubts crowded back. "There's been some mistake then," she said regretfully. It had been a beautiful fantasy for a few moments.

"There's no mistake," Rian insisted. "I wondered at first, when I first got your emails. I thought it was just that you were funny and clever and that I *liked* you, but it got stronger and stronger. I couldn't stop thinking about you. And I knew...I knew you needed me."

Tania felt her hackles rise. "I don't need you," she insisted. It was bad enough that she wanted him so wantonly that he could probably tell without the help of a magical spell, but the idea of *needing* him put up all of her walls. "I am doing fine."

It sounded like a lie to her own ears, and she knew she

hadn't convinced him, either, still sitting there with his hand being ignored between them.

Eventually, he took it back, looking puzzled and disappointed. "So, ah. You aren't working at the university library anymore?"

Curiously, Tania saw the pang of her own grief in his face. "They terminated my employment for too many missed days. Since I wasn't a student at the university any longer, what with my thesis suddenly being...sunk...I had to work enough hours this semester to be full time or they couldn't keep me on."

Rian looked guilty and scowled. "They wouldn't give you the hours?"

"I couldn't *work* the hours they gave me." Tania tamped down the familiar shame and frustration; those were certainly her own, non-magical feelings. "No employer wants an employee who has to take a day off for every full day that they work." She tried to say it lightly and failed; being fired was still a fresh shame.

It was hard not to stare at Rian, at all the expressions that crossed his handsome face. Mostly there was confusion, which Tania could keenly appreciate.

"Why can't you work a full day? I don't understand."

Tania wrenched her gaze from Rian's and stared at the table between them. "I don't know," she said wretchedly. "No one knows. Chronic fatigue? Fibromyalgia? Arthritis? Some delightful cocktail of several things at once? It's hard to get a solid diagnosis when you can't get appointments for six months and your health insurance won't cover most tests. Not that I even have that, now." She didn't mention the fact that she had burned through some of her savings to get no answers whatsoever.

"Why didn't you tell me?" Rian asked plaintively. "What can I do?"

Tania stopped herself from looking up at him. She felt a little less overwhelmingly cotton-candy perfect-happiness when she wasn't looking directly at him. This spell was *anything* but subtle. She was surprised there weren't pastel sparkles and rainbows in the air between them.

"Overhaul the health care system?" Tania suggested sarcastically. "Give me a different body?"

"Come with me."

"What, and leave all this?" She had to look up at him then, to gauge his seriousness—and he undoubtedly was. Her breath stuck in her throat because in that brief study of the kitchen table she had managed to forget how utterly beautiful he was. He was more impressive in person than any candid photo on the Internet. Even the nude ones.

"Come back with me to Alaska. Marry me. I can get you the best doctors, anything you need."

He was so earnest, so confident, that Tania had to fight back tears because the idea that a prince could sweep in and save her from her own life sounded so beautiful and easy.

"There's been a mistake," she repeated.

"This isn't a mistake," Rian insisted. He was restless in his chair, like he was trying to not to get up and loom over her.

Tania half-wished he would, so she'd have an excuse to be frightened of him. She *should* be frightened, with this tall, strong man who'd hired an investigator to hunt her down sitting in her apartment, and she simply *wasn't*. "If it's not a mistake, it's a really elaborate joke, and I don't appreciate being the butt of it."

Rian's brow furrowed in confusion, as Tania struggled with her impulse to believe every word and give him every benefit of the doubt. Magic? *Dragons?* Didn't it make a sick kind of sense that he had softened her up via email, encouraging her wildest theories. Hadn't she even been the one to suggest, mockingly, that the document was referencing *real* dragons and spells? Maybe she'd given him the idea for the deception herself.

"It's not a joke," he said quietly.

She couldn't make sense of his purpose; it seemed too far-fetched to be the kind of thing you'd spring on one of those television surprise shows, and she couldn't figure out where he might have smuggled a camera. Was it just some kind of personal kink, torturing some gullible librarian for kicks?

She had to wrestle against her instinct—which must be wrong—to trust him without reservation, even while it warred with her own common sense.

He was watching her avidly, and Tania wondered what he read on her face. She put on her pretend face. Pretend she wasn't struggling. Pretend she wasn't yearning for all of this to be real and true when it clearly could not be.

"Tania," Rian said carefully, "will you come to Alaska and marry me?"

Tania had to playact as hard as she was capable of that his words had no effect on her. Her heart wanted to soar at the idea, at the sheer inconceivable, crazy possibility of it. "No," she said firmly. "Don't be absurd."

That was clearly not the answer that Rian had expected, and Tania thought he might have felt her real reaction. He blinked rapidly in confusion. "I...er..."

"Listen to yourself!" Tania felt like all the emotion was rising up in her like a kettle with a screaming whistle. "We just met in person for the first time, and in all those emails, you never bothered to tell me that you were the prince of Alaska, let alone a *dragon*. You let me believe that you didn't know what the Compact really was, supposing it even is what you say. You *lied...*"

"I never lied—"

"If you think a lie of omission is any tiny bit better than an outright falsehood, you aren't the man I thought you were," Tania snarled.

And then, because he really was the man she thought he was, Rian immediately agreed. "You're right," he said contritely. "I had reasons for not telling you all of the truth, but I wish that I had anyway. I am genuinely *sorry* I didn't tell you sooner. I'm *sorry* that I have to live a life of deception and secrecy, and I am *sorry* that I have to ask you to be involved in that. How can I make it right?"

Tania focused on the gold stars on the collar of his uniform coat. His eyes, almost silver, were too intense to bear, and his apology was from the heart. She knew it without the slightest doubt.

More gently yet, Rian went on. "I know that you are for me, without reservation or hesitation, and I will never lie to you, by omission or otherwise, again. Please say that you will marry me."

It was a trap. Tania knew too many fairy tales to assume there wasn't a pitfall here, a trick, some deception. Perhaps it was like fairy gold, and the promise would turn to ashes in the morning once she'd given him...what did she have to give him, really? What purpose was there in her humiliation?

"No," she said, and it took all of her will. No spell, no rush of longing, no promises of riches and royalty were going to force her to act recklessly and live her life in regret.

"Oh," Rian said, in the tiniest voice that could come from someone so splendidly large. Then he laughed, helplessly and full of surrender, took off his glasses, and rubbed them off on a corner of his jacket. "You know, in literature, the heroine is usually a lot more agreeable to the prince's generous offer."

All of Tania's anger vanished in the face of his plaintive humility and it took all of her self-control not to burst out laughing. "I'm not the heroine in most literature."

"You're better," he said, with what Tania decided could be grudging admiration. "What would you have me do, then? Will you set me three impossible tasks? Will you permit me to court you? I could bring you books..." He glanced around knowingly at Tania's book-lined walls.

Tania's resolve stiffened. "I'm not letting you buy my hand. Not even with books."

"With books and cinnamon hot chocolate?"

Tania was alarmed for a moment until she remembered that she had once told him about her weakness for cinnamon and chocolate. She'd told him so many details of her life, so many tiny confessions. But...she'd never told him some of the bigger things, like how sick she was.

She sighed. "Rian..."

"What do you need?" he asked plaintively. "Anything, ask it."

"I need time," Tania admitted. "This is a lot to take in, and you're asking me to believe in six impossible things before breakfast."

"We're all mad, here." Rian had picked up the Alice in Wonderland reference at once, and it seemed remarkably apt for how Tania felt like she'd fallen down some kind of crazy rabbit hole.

3

Rian hadn't been prepared for a 'no.'

He hadn't really been prepared for anything.

He thought Tania might not *believe* him, and he thought she might be angry with him for being, indirectly, the cause of the failure of her thesis.

But surely, when they finally met, she would see that they would be happy together, that they were right together, more right than any two people had any reason to hope for.

She had flirted with him in the emails, before she even knew what he looked like, or that he was a prince, let alone a dragon. And Rian knew he wasn't *bad* looking; his identical twin brother, Tray, was convinced enough of that for both of them.

She wants us, but rebuffs us? His dragon, more susceptible to the influence of magic than Rian's human part, was unshakably certain that Tania was their destiny, and was even more baffled than Rian at her measured refusal.

What did normal people do when their marriage

proposals were turned down? Going into a crazy rage was out of character, and weeping seemed unlikely to get him any further. "May I take you out to dinner?" Possibly he should have started with that and tried to woo her a little first before dropping all the craziest details of his existence on her. It just...felt like he already knew her.

Tania looked at him in silence for a moment, then nodded, as if she was too exhausted to argue.

"Tonight?" Rian offered. "I remember that you love spicy Indian food..."

Her eyes softened a little. "You remember a lot about me."

"I reread all of your emails, so many times," he said honestly.

Color flushed into her tawny skin.

"Not a stalker," he repeated. "I just..."

"I read yours over, too." Her voice was low and if Rian had not had the sharpened senses of a dragon shifter he might not have heard it. His heart leapt in his chest.

"Tania..." Rian ached to reach for her.

"Tonight," she said, and for one blissful moment, Rian thought she'd been responding to his desire. But no, her tone was dismissive. She meant *dinner*. He'd invited her to *dinner*.

"Tonight," he agreed, getting to his feet. She didn't offer to stand, and Rian thought he felt exhaustion through their strange magical bond, but it was tangled with a hundred other sensations and emotions.

"Are you...?"

"I'm fine," she said firmly. "You can pick me up at six." She still didn't make a move to stand, or to see Rian to the door.

He paused, then knelt at her feet so he could gaze up

into her face. "Tania. It is a truth universally acknowledged…"

She burst into laughter, and her face, which Rian had not thought could grow more beautiful, was somehow dearer and deeper.

"Are you a single man in possession of good fortune?" she teased him back. "Because I am *not* the wife that you are seeking."

"I know that you are." But Rian stood, rather than arguing. "I will see you at six." He bowed courteously and saw himself out without letting himself look back.

The hallway to her apartment was muggy and narrow and dirty, but Rian felt buoyant and confident as he pulled his phone from his pocket. Tania was everything he'd expected, and more, with that hint of pain and steel behind her soft exterior. He was sure that whatever magic might be at work, he could not have asked for a more perfect partner or a more complete heart. She would come around, and he would take her to Alaska and she would be his…queen.

Rian frowned then, and paused with his finger on the button to call Tray.

It *was* unexpected that the Compact had tapped two queens, and more unexpected that it had drawn Toren, his youngest brother, to his mate Carina before an older brother, if it was going to do that. Perhaps strangest of all was that Fask, the oldest and clearly the most suited for being king, had *not* found a mate. If they had expected another mate to be called, it would have been for Fask.

Rian didn't particularly wish to be a king, though he suspected that he disliked the idea slightly less than his youngest brother Toren did. The poor kid didn't complain, but the panic in his eyes whenever the topic of *ruling* came up was obvious to anyone who knew him.

Rian pressed the button thoughtfully and brought the phone to his ear as he wandered towards the stairwell. He'd landed on the roof when he arrived, but he went down the stairs this time.

"Tray's pizza delivery," his twin answered casually.

"I'm calling for a pie of humility," Rian said dryly.

"Oh, yeah, did you meet your long-distance love? Did the world shake beneath your feet?"

Rian had to smile foolishly, remembering how it had felt to finally see her. "You could say that."

Tray was quiet. "So, wait…"

"She's my mate. No doubts."

Rian knew that if they'd been face-to-face, he would have seen a mirror of his own features, blinking in surprise the same way that he tended to. He pushed his glasses up on his nose self-consciously.

"So…you're bringing home a bride? Are you thinking about some kind of double wedding with our baby brother?"

"Well, ah…" Rian abruptly remembered that Tania had said no. "We're not there yet."

"I thought you said there were no doubts." Tray's voice took a note of skepticism.

"Not on *my* part," Rian said reluctantly.

As he'd anticipated, Tray cackled. "She turned you *down?*"

"I'm sure it was a bit of a shock!" Rian protested. "Dragons and magic, and…I'm not sure she's quite forgiven me for being involved, however distantly, in the torpedoing of her thesis."

Tray was still laughing, sounding far away, as if he wasn't capable of holding his phone near his face.

"I'm taking her to dinner tonight," Rian said sullenly.

"And you called for some dating tips?" Tray teased.

"No." Rian was suddenly not sure why he'd called. He couldn't exactly ask them to prepare for the arrival of a woman who'd made no indication that she had any interest in returning with him. He'd mostly just wanted to share his elation, the feeling of contentment and joy that meeting Tania had sparked in his heart. "No," he said. He should have called Toren, he thought wryly. Toren, of all of his brothers, would appreciate what he was going through.

After all, Carina had outright fled when they met. Rian should count his blessings that Tania hadn't. Though he suspected that fleeing was out of character...and maybe not even possible. He had been surprised by her condition, caught completely flat-footed. She had mentioned being tired a few times in their emails, but he hadn't expected her to be struggling with her health. What else didn't he know?

"I guess I just wanted to give you a heads-up," Rian said.

"Should I tell Fask?"

Rian hesitated. "Not yet."

"Does this make you the crown prince, instead of Toren?" Tray asked, exactly as Rian circled back to that question himself.

"Toren found his mate first," Rian pointed out. "That...probably means something?"

"Maybe the Compact realized it had made a terrible mistake," Tray said, but he said it in a way that was more thoughtful than mocking. They had all been surprised and impressed by how well Toren had stepped up to the challenge. "Anyway, it's all a moot point if you don't woo the girl, so you'd better get your courting pants on and practice your poetry. What time is it there?"

Poetry. She *did* like poetry. Rian looked at his watch. "It's almost ten in the morning."

He could guess that Tray was scowling. "You woke me

up before six AM to rub in the fact that your pen pal was your mate?"

"There was a good chance that you were facing the morning from the other end of the day," Rian pointed out.

Tray chuckled. "Point. What's your plan of attack?"

"I pick her up at six," Rian said. "I'll take her to the nicest Indian restaurant in the area."

"Taxi? Limo? A bicycle built for two?"

Rian hadn't thought that far ahead. "Ah, a limo?"

"Got a company lined up? It's Friday, they might not have last-minute availability. You got a good suit to wear?"

"I'm wearing my uniform."

"Oh, that's subtle," Tray scoffed.

"I didn't exactly pack to come down here," Rian said. He'd barely taken the time to change clothes, before impulsively flying nearly five thousand miles on his own wings. His shoulders still ached slightly.

"Do you have a hotel lined up?" Tray prodded. "Where do you plan to take her afterwards?"

"I…" Rian hadn't even considered what would happen next.

"This is unlike you, little brother," Tray teased. "Aren't you usually the one who is scheduled to the minute? I suppose you called the credit card company to let them know you'd be making purchases in Florida so they don't block you for fraud when you try to pay for your date?"

"I…ah…" Rian patted his pockets in sudden alarm.

"Did you at least bring a copy of your diplomatic passport?" Tray sighed.

Rian gave a groan.

"No passport?" Tray guessed.

"I forgot my wallet."

Tray really did drop his phone then; Rian could hear him chortling as he fumbled for it.

"Done laughing?" Rian wanted to know.

"Probably not," Tray admitted.

"Can you mail it by courier to me, with my passport?" Rian asked, knowing already that he was never going to live this down.

"It won't be there in time for your date," Tray predicted. "You'll need some cash."

"I suppose you have some idea where I might get some?" Rian was sure that his brother had been caught flat-footed before.

"I do indeed," Tray said. The delight in his voice filled Rian with dread.

4

Tania's apartment was small and dingy, and it seemed smaller and dingier after Rian left. After a few moments, she got up, detouring for her cane, and locked the door behind him.

Then she leaned weakly against the door and tried to make sense out of what had just happened.

Rian, *here*.

An Alaskan prince, even more handsome than his photographs, because he'd *smiled* at her. Smiled like the sun and the moon and like she'd hung them both.

And if that was not unbelievable enough, he'd all but opened the door to faerie for her.

Magic. Dragons. *Mates.*

His mate. She was *his mate*.

She shouldn't believe a word of it. It was too inconceivable to stand.

But somehow, everything that he explained fell into perfectly sensible patterns, filling in all the little gaps of logic that had always been there.

Tania screwed her eyes shut, thinking about her lost

thesis, about the theories that she hadn't been able to commit to paper, only to the emails to Rian filled with wild speculation.

After a few moments, she pushed off from the door and went to the kitchen sink. She systematically emptied the drainer, then filled the sink with soapy water. Washing dishes made her feel anchored again. Cleaning in general did, so when she was finished with the dishes, she tidied the counters and cleared old take-out containers from the refrigerator and tied the trash up by the door, and then, because her mind was still busy and she could not make her thoughts stop circling, she scrubbed out the bathtub.

She only realized what a mistake it was when she tried to rise from wiping the last of the suds from the drain.

She'd been so busy thinking, imagining Rian's beautiful face, wondering what it would feel like to brush his hair back from his forehead, that she hadn't noticed how hard she had thrown herself into the cleaning.

The cane had been left in the kitchen, her hands full of toxic supplies, and Tania had to use the towel rack to regain her feet. It groaned in protest, and for a moment, Tania was afraid it would come out under her weight and send her tumbling back to the floor.

Her whole body protested the work she'd done. Her arms ached, and her worst hip was on fire. Every joint was filing objections, and her fingers and feet tingled threateningly.

"No," Tania said firmly. "Just, no."

She made herself eat lunch, a serving of yogurt because anything else required cooking and even putting something in the microwave felt like too much work. She took the maximum dose of her over-the-counter meds and eyed her prescriptions in frank dismay when the others still weren't working an hour later. She couldn't go to dinner in this much pain. But the pain-killers would leave her too loopy to even make conversation.

Look like an idiot because she could barely speak around the discomfort of sitting? Or look like an idiot because her brain was wrapped in cotton?

She forced herself through her physical therapy and stretching, and lay down for a nap hoping desperately to regain some of her strength.

Sleep resisted her, driven away by discomfort, and she finally rose, weeping, to gather her phone from the charger, squinting around the familiar headache that was blooming.

She turned it on to find the expected missed calls from her mother...and a whole series of calls from an unknown international number.

Rian.

He had left some voicemails that Tania didn't feel equal to listening to, but she stared at the notifications for a long while before she poked out a short text to the number.

I can't go out tonight, sorry. Maybe tomorrow. She sent it before she could agonize over the tone or whether she should explain. There was no way she'd found to expound that didn't sound like she wasn't complaining, and she *hated* complaining.

Sorry! she added impulsively. Would a smiley face make it better, or worse, she wondered.

Then she turned her phone off, took the maximum dose from her dwindling supply of pills, and crawled into bed to weep in frustration and pain until she could finally sleep.

∽

Tania woke an unknown period of time later, dizzy and confused, but no longer controlled by pain.

It would have been inaccurate to say that she wasn't in pain—it still lurked around all the edges of her, grabbing at her every nerve-ending and thought. Even the roots of her hair hurt. But she was distant from it, safely apart from her earlier agony.

Something had woken her, and after a while, she slowly realized that someone was knocking on her door.

She rose carefully, using her cane this time.

Her clothing was rumpled, and she never had been able to brush her hair that morning, but the pills kept her from caring about that like they kept her from caring about her discomfort.

She unlocked the chain and opened the door slowly, already knowing who she'd find. "Rian."

He looked every bit as handsome and earnest as he had before, and no pill in the world could keep Tania's heart from leaping at the sight of him.

"You said in your text that you couldn't go out," he said hesitantly, lifting two huge take-out bags. "But you didn't say that you didn't want to see me."

Tania just stared for a moment, because she *had* wanted to see him. Desperately. Like there was a magical compulsion driving her, against all sense and all normalcy.

He remained in the hallway, not offering to come in when she didn't invite him. "I found the best Indian restaurant in town, according to Yelp. I wasn't sure what you liked best, so I got a little of everything. Garlic naan, and biryani, and some things I don't even know. Spicy hot. We don't have a lot of Indian food in Fairbanks. Seventeen kinds of Thai, though. And if you want, I'll hire an Indian chef. Or an Italian chef. You said you liked that, too."

Tania realized that he was babbling, and that she was still standing in her doorway staring stupidly at him. If *he* was real, couldn't *magic* be real?

She finally stepped aside, and he came in. "I'm sorry," she said, not sure which part of her life she was apologizing for.

"Please don't be," Rian said sincerely as he carried the bags to the counter. "I honestly hate going out to restaurants. All the silverware and the wine menus and people trying to look like they aren't taking photos of me on their phones. Oh, I got a bottle of wine. But we don't have to open it."

"I shouldn't," Tania said. "I had to take some medicine. It doesn't mix well."

"No wine," Rian said cheerfully, unpacking his bags and opening steaming containers. "But I did also get chocolate ice cream for dessert. Can I put this in your freezer? I'm not really...dressed for your weather, so something cold sounded good. When I left, it was about fifteen degrees and we'd already gotten a foot of snow. I didn't even think about the fact that it would be hot in Florida."

"Snow?" Tania said stupidly, thinking about how flattering his uniform was. "In October? I think of October as fall."

"This is your fall?" Rian exclaimed. "I passed a thermometer that said ninety."

"It's as low as fifty at night," Tania pointed out. "That's an improvement." She finally realized what was bothering her about his uniform and her manners were too muffled by her medicine to keep herself from saying, "Eight stars of gold. What happened to your button?"

One of the gold stars at his neck was missing. There was even a faint thread still there.

Rian, adorably, *blushed*. "I pawned it," he confessed. "I left in a hurry to fly here as a dragon, and I forgot my wallet at home."

Something tickled the back of Tania's throat and when she opened her mouth, she realized it was a laugh.

5

If Rian had not been standing right next to her to catch her by the arm, he was sure that Tania would have fallen over laughing, cane and all.

"What's so funny?" he asked. He might have asked crossly, but it was impossible to feel cross when he was gently holding her upright as she shook in mirth.

"A prince of Alaska just pawned his *button* to buy me dinner," Tania pointed out, and when she said it that way, Rian could not resist laughing with her.

"I told you," he reminded her. "Not much of the princely image. Are you hungry? Because I paid a good gold button for this food."

"I'm starving," Tania admitted. Rian, still holding her arm, helped her to a seat at the table, where she leaned her cane beside her on the chair.

He rummaged through her cabinets and found plates and utensils, then gave her a heaped serving of everything, over her protests that it was too much, that she'd never have room for it all. His own plate was just as full, and he was happy to dig in with her, his uniform jacket hanging from the back of his chair.

"I'm not going to be a great conversationalist," Tania warned him. "The stuff I took makes my head muddy."

"We don't have to talk about anything serious," Rian told her. "Have you read the latest book by Saia Jones?"

"Ah!" Tania said in outrage. "No spoilers! I've got it requested at the library but it's not in yet."

Rian mimed zipping his mouth shut. "I won't tell," he promised. But he couldn't resist adding, "But the big reveal is worth the wait."

Tania bared her teeth at him threateningly, then laughed and they settled into eating and talking easily about books. Rian tried not to stare too hard while they ate, or let the fascinating planes of her face distract him from their conversation.

She looked up and caught him watching her as she chased the last bit of curry with a scrap of naan. "I hope my emails didn't give you a...false impression," she said shyly.

"What? No. How could they? You're..." She was perfect. Brilliant. Beautiful.

"Broken?"

"Broken? I was going to say beautiful."

He could feel her wrestling with the mixture of pleasure and embarrassment and skepticism that his words caused. "Kind of you to say so, Your Highness."

"Well, I'm certainly not disappointed," Rian said firmly, not sure how to argue the point. He could see how she was fighting back pain, could *feel* how she was holding herself together from sheer force of will. "Are you?" he thought to add. "Disappointed, I mean?"

Tania nearly choked on the naan. "Disappointed that you turned out to be a prince?" she laughed. "Or that you also happen to be able to change into a dragon?" Her eyes took on a dreamy, happy gleam. "You brought me the knowledge that there is magic in our world, and I could never be disappointed by that." Her gaze sharpened. "But I do have some questions," she said firmly.

"With dessert?" Rian said hopefully. "How is it still eight hundred degrees this late?" The combination of heat and humidity and hot food was making him sweat. He really should have thought about his destination when he dressed, but he'd only been concerned with *impressing* her.

It worked, his dragon reminded him. Sometimes, Rian thought that his dragon was his vanity.

Tania leaned over to view the thermostat. "Whiner. It's only seventy-nine." Then she looked abashed. "Your Highness," she added.

"You don't have to call me Your Highness," Rian said, gathering their plates. "Please, don't." He remembered where the bowls were from his previous cabinet search and bent a spoon in the hard ice cream before Tania pointed out the drawer with an ice cream scoop. He bent the spoon back into shape and sheepishly rifled through the drawer for the scoop. By the time he found it, tangled up with a potato masher and a whisk, the ice cream was softer, and he heaped their bowls full of the dark chocolate dessert.

"What *should* I call you?" Tania asked seriously, taking the bowl.

My love, Rian wanted to say. *Or darling. Or...husband.*

Mate, his dragon supplied simply. *We are hers.*

"Rian," he finally decided. "Just Rian."

"Alright, *just-Rian*," Tania teased him. Then her eyes shut as she took a bite of her ice cream. "What brand is this ambrosia?" she demanded, licking her lips.

"I had the Ritz-Carlton pack me a pint from their

restaurant," Rian said with a shrug. "I don't know what it is."

"You're staying at the Ritz-Carlton?" Tania's eyebrows went to vanish in her over-long fringe. "Geez, pawning a royal button really does go a long way."

Rian blushed. "Ah, well, I had my brother call in with a credit card for that one. I didn't have my photo ID, and I'm pretty sure the desk clerk didn't believe me when I said who I was, but a manager recognized me. Well, not me, he thought I was Tray, but...it worked out. I got a room." Rian had remembered Tray's advice, and booked the hotel's penthouse, but he hadn't really planned to take Tania there.

Unless she *wanted* to...Rian had to force his thoughts away from the idea, watching her lick chocolate from her lips after a particularly heaping spoonful.

Tania looked at him with a long dubious expression before shaking her head in disbelief. "Magic," she said wonderingly. "Dragons."

"Mates," Rian couldn't resist adding. He put his own spoonful of ice cream into his mouth.

"The magic..." Tania said slowly. "Is it spells and chanting? Are we talking Belgariad where it's just willpower and focus? Shannara or Middle-Earth with magic-imbued objects? Harry Potter with spells and components?" She stirred what remained of her ice cream, melting fast. "Wicca, with the nude moon ceremonies?" She'd always been drawn to books with fantastical elements, and magic fascinated her most of all.

Rian gave a chuckle. "Sort of...not any of them? I mean, it requires will. And a caster has to write it out, but it's not memorized formulas, they can write anything, as long as it's really specific, because it can get chaotic if it's not directed correctly."

Tania nodded sagely. "Magic and mythology often have tricksters as a core component."

"And I'm starting to think that the Compact is the greatest trickster of all," Rian said.

"And the Compact is not just a treaty, it's a spell? A seven-hundred page spell dictating trade and succession and policies between all of the Small Kingdoms? A spell that *enforces* compliance?"

Rian nodded. "Mm-hm."

"You realize how crazy that sounds."

"You proposed it to me yourself."

"Facetiously! Because of all the parts that didn't otherwise make sense!" Tania protested. "Will you judge me if I lick my bowl?"

Rian proved he wouldn't by lifting his own bowl to laughingly lick out the last of the sweet, cool cream and she followed suit.

He lowered his bowl and watched her, her eyes closed in pleasure, her...tongue, her page-callused fingers around the plastic bowl.

She opened her eyes and she caught his gaze before he could lower it.

"'*They will know each other as if they know themselves,*'" she said thoughtfully, putting her bowl down. "'*And they shall glimpse that to be after.*' I believe you now because I'm *going* to believe you."

"Toren said that he and Carina felt...what they were going to feel, before it really grew naturally between them," Rian said hesitantly. "And each other, that they *felt* each other. What the other one was feeling. For a little while, anyway. Spells fade."

Tania winced. "I'm sorry for that, then," she said bitterly. "But I'm glad it's only for a little while. Does it go away quickly?"

It took Rian a moment to understand that she meant. "I'm not sorry. This..." he gestured at her cane, and the tidy row of prescription bottles on the counter, "it's part of who you are. I wish I could take it from you, but I'm not sorry to know what it's like."

Tania's eyes were hollow, but tearless. "How much of it do you...get?"

Rian considered. "I feel like I'm sitting on something desperately uncomfortable, not sharp pain, just dull, heavy, and heavier still because it feels so inevitable."

Tania bowed her head and Rian could feel the confused grief from her. "What about you?" he asked gently. "What do you feel from me?"

Tania's dark eyes were glittering and deep when she lifted her gaze to his. "You *want* me," she said, and the air became charged between them. She said it again, in wonder. "You want *me*."

6

Tania had a keen imagination, and she had read a vast array of romance books that ranged from classical to absolutely trashy. She'd even had a serious boyfriend, and thought she understood what love was. He'd gotten bored as she'd gotten sicker, not satisfied with the energy she could spare him, and she'd spent a heart-broken month wondering what else she could have done to keep him.

But none of her romances, real or fictional, had prepared her for this.

Tania tried to filter out the fog in her brain from the curious swirl of emotions that weren't her own. Magic seemed like the tiniest part of the impossibility of all of this.

It wasn't just that Rian was absolutely gorgeous, though he certainly was. And it wasn't that he was built, even though he had a physique that was obvious through the fine, white shirt that he'd been wearing under the thick blue uniform coat. Being a prince had abstract appeal, but it wasn't honestly even in his top ten qualities.

He loved books, like she did. He could sit quietly, like she could. He held the values she did. He was smart, and funny, and willing to listen. He was courteous, and his voice was calm and deep and smooth.

And he *got* her.

He understood why she was frustrated, without pitying her. He'd seen her arsenal of medical crutches, watched her hobble on her cane. He knew that she'd been fired, and had lost her purpose and prospects when her academic career fell down around her.

And even knowing everything, all her weakness and all her failures, he still *wanted* her.

His desire wasn't just physical, but it was that, too, and Tania was absolutely lost in her own wanton wishes. She wanted his touch, his kiss, she wanted to thread her hands into his hair—it looked just long enough to curl over her fingers. She wanted him to lay her down right here on the kitchen table in an act of animal need, even knowing how uncomfortable it would be.

"You have chocolate on your face," she said, and it was exactly the excuse she needed to reach across the table with her napkin to dab it off.

His breath caught in his throat as she touched him, and she was watching him so closely she could see the muscles in his jaw tighten and the tendons in his neck leap out. She wiped the corner of his mouth, fascinated with how his lips moved as he licked his lips reflexively and swallowed.

She let her thumb slip past the napkin and touch his mouth, just the barest brush.

"Tania," he said, more hoarsely than he'd said anything since they met.

Tania wasn't sure how they stood up. She certainly didn't reach for her cane, and she wasn't aware of Rian coming around the table to her. She only knew that they were suddenly standing close, close enough that she could smell him, and feel the solid warmth of him, and anticipate his kiss like it was the only thing in her future.

But it didn't come.

Rian made a noise like a groan, or a balloon losing air.

"You could..." Tania invited, not even sure where she was going to take the sentence.

"I couldn't," Rian said firmly, his voice almost a growl.

There was another noise, and Tania realized that it had been hers, a whimper of need and disappointment.

"You've taken mind-altering medication," Rian reminded her. "If I took advantage of that..."

"It wouldn't really be taking advantage," Tania protested. She was all but throwing herself at him, wasn't she? It was a little hard to sort through all the things she was feeling. That *he* was feeling. That *they were going to feel*.

"I can wait," Rian said, and the resolve in his voice made Tania wonder if she ought to be feeling ashamed of herself. "I can wait as long as I need to. As long as you need."

Tania sighed, and sagged in place a little. Rian, perhaps fearing she was going to fall, caught her up his arms and held her, and Tania tipped her head up, thinking she might get her kiss after all.

And she did, but it was a chaste kiss to her forehead, just the barest of pressure from his mouth before he was lowering her back down into her chair and all the discomfort in her body that she'd forgotten about for a moment was back.

Disappointment was bitter, but some dispassionate part of Tania's mind pointed out that he had only managed to be more perfect, and that she'd probably be glad of it in the morning.

She was also more than a little worried that she

wouldn't ever be brave enough again, and that she had lost her only chance to make sweet, sweaty love to a dragon prince. She made herself shake her head and laugh.

"Let me wash these up for you," Rian said, gathering up their spoons and bowls.

"You don't have to wash my dishes," Tania scolded him.

"Do you *want* to do them?" Rian asked frankly.

Her medicine made her honest. "Not in the slightest," she confessed. She usually found cleaning to be a grounding activity, but she had only the barest stores of energy left now, and she didn't relish the task.

"Then I will wash them," Rian said boldly before she could add that they would wait until morning. He carried the dishes to the counter. "You have...ah...soap? Oh, here's a *sponge.*" He gave it a mystified squeeze.

"Have you ever washed dishes in your life?" Tania pointed out the dispenser above the drainer, which was already full of dishes.

"Not once," Rian admitted cheerfully as he rolled up the sleeves of his fine white shirt. He swiftly realized that he'd need to make room in the drainer, and Tania directed him from her chair to where everything went away.

Then he filled up the sink with soapy water—a little too much soapy water, so that it splashed everywhere whenever he added a dish. He was careful with her dishes, and a little overwhelmed. His hands were too big to get into her glasses, and watching him try to stuff the sponge into them put Tania into near-hysterical peals of laughter.

He was comically bad at the task, nearly overflowing the sink when he went to rinse, fumbling with the strainer and then unable to get it back in soundly and losing all of his water while he worked with unnecessarily detail on the space between fork tines.

"This sounds easier than it actually is," he said, turning back to her at last, and his white shirt was so wet and soaked to his chest that Tania was incapable of words.

"Ah blah dah…" she managed. Could she blame that on her medicine? She blushed and failed to stop staring. "I...uh...thank you for washing my dishes. It was very kind of you."

A prince, she reminded herself. A dragon-shifting prince had washed her dishes. No part of that sentence made much sense at all. A dragon. A prince. A gorgeous guy *washing her dishes*. She circled back to the idea that he was a *dragon*, as the most impossible part. Or maybe the part where he thought she was his *chosen mate* was the most impossible part.

"I should go," Rian said awkwardly. "Can I do anything else for you?"

Tania could think of several things. "No," she said simply. "You've done so much."

Rian dabbed useless at his shirt with an already soaked dishtowel and gave up on it. "Tomorrow. Can I see you tomorrow?" He stepped past her to get his jacket and Tania was struck by how much space he took up in her tiny apartment.

"Yes," she said too quickly, reaching for her cane. "I mean...yes. Please. But maybe my treat, so you don't have to pawn the rest of your buttons and leave yourself naked." It was ridiculous, offering to pay for a *prince*. She wasn't terribly dismayed by the idea of him naked, however.

"Coffee?" Rian suggested. "You said there was a cafe you liked to read at in the morning, just down the street."

"Magic Beans," Tania said, standing carefully. "It seems apt. It won't be very early," she warned. "I tend to crash after days like this."

It was weird to be so frank about it, but it felt...nice.

"Ten?"

"Ten," Tania agreed.

For an awkward moment, neither of them was sure what to do.

Then Rian swooped in, gave her another swift, unfortunately-chaste forehead kiss, and bustled out, leaving Tania feeling unexpectedly bereft.

7

"You're in the penthouse of the Ritz-Carlton. By yourself."

"It has a great view," Rian told his twin. It really did, with a picturesque lake and the sparkling city beyond. Certainly, it was better than the view out of Tania's living room window, which was basically the wall of another apartment building.

"So...dinner didn't go that great?" Tray didn't sound as surprised as Rian thought he should.

"Dinner was nice." Just talking to Tania, sharing food, watching her enjoyment in the Indian takeout and the chocolate ice cream, her animated face when she talked about the books she loved...Rian thought that *nice* was an understatement, but knew that his brother would never understand.

"Nice." Tray was thoroughly unimpressed.

"It was...nice." Her bare arms in his hands, her bright eyes. Her face, tipped up for the kiss he couldn't give her. "She was...incapacitated."

Rian could hear Tray rubbing his head, and a dog barked in the background. "She was incapacitated?"

"There are...complications."

"There would be," Tray said dryly. "Is she wanted for murder?"

"Not that complicated," Rian said with a chuckle.

"Did you get her drunk?" Tray pried.

"No!" Rian said furiously. "It's..." he stopped, not sure how to proceed without violating Tania's privacy.

"So..." Tray drawled, "are you bringing her home soon?"

Soon, Rian's dragon hissed. *Soon.*

"I told you, it's complicated."

"Do you need backup?"

Rian had a moment of horror, imagining Tray meeting Tania. "No. Definitely not. Please do not come."

Tray was quiet and Rian dug down for something to distract him. Something Tray would care about. "How are Phoebe's puppies? How many were there?"

"Four!" Tray said enthusiastically. "Two girls and two boys and they're all healthy at three weeks. One of them is a bit of a runt, but she's still a fighter, right in there for the milk. Bet she'll make a great leader, she's already the sneakiest. Carina wants the other girl."

"What does Mrs. James have to say about that?"

"Carina's got Mrs. James wrapped around her little finger," Tray scoffed. "But you don't care about dogs. What are you going to do about your mate?"

Rian looked out over the glittering skyscape. "Everything," he said simply. "I'm going to do everything."

"What does this make you?" Tray asked pointedly.

"Huh?" Rian was thinking about Tania again, her loose hair and her dark eyes, her beautiful, curvy body and the way her face lit up when she spoke about something that interested her.

"Are you the crown prince now?"

Rian froze, horrified. He kept managing to forget about that particular aspect of things.

"Toren will be so relieved," Tray teased him. "He's going to think he dodged a bullet."

"Toren was doing fine," Rian said, sure that his panic was obvious in his voice. "He can be king. I don't want to be king."

"Who does?" Tray scoffed. "Well, Fask, maybe," he answered himself. "But even Fask knows what a thankless job it is."

"Have you told anyone?" Rian asked urgently.

"That you found your *mate*?" Tray laughed. "That Alaska has *two* pending queens? No, baby brother, I was going to leave that honor for you."

Rian was relieved. The longer he could put that off, the longer he could spend here, with Tania, without his family and the press putting them in the spotlight. On that note, "Where do you buy clothes?"

"What?"

"Clothes. All I brought was my uniform. It kind of stands out, besides being more suited for Alaska in October than Florida." He had a little cash from the pawn shop, still, but not a lot.

Tray dissolved into laughter at the other end of the phone. "Are you *sure* you don't need help? I could be there late tomorrow morning if I flew straight."

"No!" The last thing Rian wanted was his brother crashing his coffee date. "I just need...like a t-shirt or something."

"Call your concierge," Tray advised. "You're staying in

the penthouse, I'm sure they'd be happy to run out to the Gap and grab you something. Tip well."

Rian hadn't even thought of that. "Oh, okay. I could do that."

"Hey, little brother—" Tray said. Rian didn't even mind the reminder that he'd been born a scant few minutes later than Tray. "Congratulations. I'm happy for you."

Rian let all of his breath out. "You have no idea," he said honestly. "You have no idea how amazing it is. She's...amazing. Everything I ever wanted. Everything I ever looked for. Everything I never even knew I was looking for."

"I'm happy for you," Tray repeated, and Rian wondered if he sounded just the littlest bit jealous.

8

Tania set three alarms when she went to bed, double-checking each of them in paranoid fear that she would sleep right through her coffee date with Rian. One was on her bedside clock—an ancient green-digital thing that she'd had since high school, one was on her phone, and one was on her reading tablet.

She slept more restfully than she expected to, given the day she'd had and all of its alarming revelations, and she woke up about ten minutes before the first alarm began to chime. She spent that time staring at her ceiling, thinking about Rian, and replaying their memory-muddied conversation and their almost-kiss.

The first alarm had her flinging back her light comforter, testing her limbs cautiously. To her relief, she was feeling considerably better; her shower was almost easy, daydreaming about Rian's clever fingers as she tried not to get too distracted soaping herself. She ate a single-serve yogurt, so she wouldn't get too dizzy from hunger and caffeine, and she even brushed her hair.

Styling it was still beyond her, though she lifted the

ends a few times and frowned at the grown-out highlights. Lately, it had been an expense, and an expenditure of energy, that she simply hadn't been able to spare.

There was no fixing it now, so Tania sighed, tucked her tablet into her purse, and eyed her cane with distaste.

She didn't *want* to take it, but she knew that her morning flexibility could vanish without warning, triggered by stepping wrong off a sidewalk, or sitting too long in an unpadded chair. She might trip, or simply seize up for no discernible reason, and she didn't want to be caught without its assistance.

Then she thought that Rian might just carry her home, and the idea both mortified her and made her feel weak enough in the knees that she picked up the cane with less resignation than before.

She got to the cafe well before ten, giving herself more time than strictly necessary to make the two-block walk.

The barista gave her a surprised look. "We haven't seen you for a while! Mocha with a shot of cinnamon dulce?"

Tania gave her a slow smile, grateful that she'd been remembered and missed. She'd seen her termination coming, and coffee out had become one of those precious treats that she couldn't indulge in like she wished she could.

Then she remembered that a prince had offered to marry her and she added a six dollar tip to her credit card. The barista drew hearts all over her cup and bubbled over in joy.

Only after Tania had settled into one of her favorite tables and pulled out her tablet did she think to wonder how she was going to pay for Rian's drink. Was she supposed to get up and stand with him in line again? Should she have loitered without putting in her own order until he got there? What *was* the social convention?

She was still agonizing over what to do when she spotted him on the sidewalk outside and her heart did little backflips of excitement.

He was wearing a faded dark t-shirt that looked stiff with newness; it must be artistically distressed. His blue jeans did even more for his body than his uniform had, and Tania waved shyly when he came into the cafe. He was carrying a book.

He ignored the line for coffee entirely, and all the stares he was getting, and came to sit across from Tania. "You got here early," he said ruefully. "I thought I'd beat you."

Tania smiled at him foolishly. "I didn't want to be late."

She wasn't sure how long they smiled at each other without speaking, but she guessed that they looked pretty ridiculous.

"Um, coffee," Rian said at last, shaking his head.

"Oh, it's my treat," Tania said, and she pulled out her purse to give him a ten-dollar bill, feeling triumphant for finding a solution. Rian left his book on the table and went to stand in line.

Tania pretended to read and watched him over the top of her tablet.

He was so effortlessly elegant, so tall and unknowingly commanding. Everyone who glanced at him gave a long second look. He didn't invite conversation, but he did smile and nod politely when anyone got too close. She didn't think any of them actually recognized him; no one was expecting to see a prince from Alaska slumming around a tiny cafe in Orlando wearing blue jeans.

The bubbly barista nearly swooned, smiling and giggling, and when Rian turned to walk to Tania's table, she met Tania's eyes from behind his back and made a show of fanning herself appreciatively.

Rian had used the money to not only buy himself a

dark coffee, but had also picked out two pastries—a chocolate croissant for Tania and a blueberry scone for himself.

"Oh, thank you," Tania said, eyeing the sweets with delight.

"No, thank *you*," Rian said courteously as he settled across from her. "It was your treat."

There was an awkward silence, then he asked, "What are you reading?" at the same moment that Tania asked, "What book is that?"

Rian out-polited her, and Tania confessed that she was re-reading an old comfort read, the Dragonriders of Pern. "It seemed...appropriate," she said shyly, and they both laughed. Tania glanced around self-consciously, but no one was paying the slightest bit of attention to them. "You?"

Rian held up a second-hand thriller. "The only thing remotely interesting in the book exchange at the hotel."

"It's a good one," Tania said, taking a bite of croissant and trying to catch her crumbs. "It's one of his early ones; he was still writing real books at that point, not phoning it in."

"You read his work?"

Tania shrugged. "Sometimes it's all there is in the book exchange."

They talked about the genre a little, which led to a critical discussion of cover choices. "I swear, they try to get the author name a little bigger on each cover," Rian scoffed. "Pretty soon, they won't even bother putting the title on the cover, just the author name in seven hundred point text."

"You'll have to guess which book it is by the color, I suppose," Tania giggled. "I loved the old eighties fantasy covers, those lush illustrations that never actually matched the descriptions of the characters."

"Lots of dragons," Rian said approvingly. "And flaming swords."

"Are...are flaming swords a thing?" Tania asked wistfully. If dragons and magic were real...

"I haven't run into any yet." Rian sounded regretful. "Nor rings of invisibility."

Tania thought longingly that Rian looked like he could have stepped right off one of the covers to a terrible romance book. Rip off the shirt a little, add some wind to ruffle his hair. She couldn't quite keep her imagination from running wild, and she quickly changed the topic.

They talked about books, laughing easily with each other, until Tania had taken a dozen sips from her already-empty cup and their pastries were reduced to crumbs.

She wasn't aware of the change in the tenor of the shop until she caught a wry expression on Rian's face and a sour sideways look. She glanced around carefully, and found that they were the subject of most of the attention in the cafe, people whispering together and watching them. Some of them looked like they were trying not to look like they were taking photos with their phones.

Someone had figured out who Rian was.

"Sorry," he mouthed at her, giving a half-shrug.

Tania wrinkled her nose at him, then wondered if someone was going to get an unflattering photo of it.

"You want to get out of here?" he offered, leaning forward.

"The library...?" Tania started to suggest by habit. "Not the University, the public one. It's just a few blocks away."

"Sounds perfect," Rian agreed. He bussed their dishes and Tania forgot that she'd brought her cane, knocking it off the back of her chair to land with a terrible clatter on the floor as she stood.

Tania froze, mortified. Before she had time to do more than color, Rian had swept back. He must have given his audience quite a show when he knelt down to get it for her. Someone giggled, but Tania wasn't sure if it was for him, or for her own keenly-felt clumsiness.

The crowd by the door melted away in front of them, some of them less circumspect about their picture-taking as Rian took Tania's arm into his elbow and sauntered out of the coffee shop.

9

They were halfway down the block away from the coffee shop before Rian realized he was walking entirely too fast for Tania. She was scrambling beside him, not a word of complaint, her cane swiftly tapping the sidewalk, but he caught a hiss of pain when she stepped wrong and her gait seemed forced.

"Sorry. I didn't think." He instantly slowed, and Tania flashed him a smile of gratitude.

"You're probably used to that," Tania said, glancing behind them.

Rian shrugged. "Not really," he confessed. "The locals know we don't like a lot of fuss, and I don't go out for diplomatic things that much. Especially lately, since Father—" He fell silent, not sure how to finish the statement.

"What...what did happen to your father?" Tania asked carefully. "The news says he's sick. Maybe in a coma?"

"He's asleep," Rian said firmly. "Fask is afraid it's the kind of sleep an old dragon never wakes from."

A passerby going the opposite direction gave them an alarmed look. Rian wasn't sure if his words had been overheard, or if they had suddenly recognized him. Most people hurried past without noticing them.

"The library is this way," Tania said, guiding him around a busy corner. "This has always been my favorite place.

"Oh," said Rian in admiration. "I can see why."

The Orlando Public Library was an impressive building, tall, intimidating, and sprawling. It was even better inside, and Rian wanted to linger and peer at the interpretive displays, but Tania pulled him forward knowingly, deeper and deeper into the stacks and nested rooms, past the children's brightly-lit room and across gleaming floors.

"This is where it all started," she told him. "They still had old microfiche files when I started, though they were already phasing it out when I found the copies of the original Compact."

They had a kiosk in the back, for historical purposes, Rian supposed, and Tania showed him how to spool the film into the viewer with a demo reel of an old newspaper. "You could pay for copies, this way," she explained, showing him where the pages printed. "It cost me three hundred and fifty bucks to print the whole damn thing. They moved to entirely electronic records the following year, when I went to college."

"You printed it in *high school?*" Rian said in astonishment. "Why would you *do* that?"

"We had to do a paper on any historic document. Most people did the Constitution, or the *Magna Carta*, or the Rosetta Stone. But I'd been reading a bunch of stuff about The Small Kingdoms, and I thought I'd impress my AP history teacher by doing some research and writing about the *original* Compact."

"Did you?" Rian asked.

"I failed the paper," Tania said wryly. "My teacher

called it highly imaginative and suggested that I pursue creative writing instead of history in college."

Rian spun the knob that flipped through the pages of microfiche, scanning the dated titles. Elections, famines, war, the price of oil, a fluff piece about a cow. "But you didn't give up."

"I didn't realize that I'd found a *secret* copy of the Compact," Tania said. Her face was lit up from the faintly green screen, and she looked distant and dreamy. "I just thought it was an *old* copy, that there had been changes to modernize the language or whatever. I went through four advisors while I was in undergrad to find one that would sponsor me and my crazy, obscure thesis about the symbolism."

Rian looked at the stubborn set of her jaw, the sweep of her dark hair around her cheeks. Her long bangs shadowed her eyes, and she wouldn't look at him.

"I'm...so sorry that your thesis got...er…"

"Yanked out from underneath me?" Tania shrugged wearily. "I don't know that I would have been able to finish it anyway." She rubbed her leg absently, then fixed Rian with an unwavering glare. "But you can make it up to me."

Anything, Rian thought in concert with his dragon.

"Tell me what it really says. Show me a copy of the real thing. Explain what it means. *All* of it. I want to *know*."

"No one understands it," Rian cautioned. "I will tell you everything I know, show you every page, answer any questions that I can. But…you'd have to come back with me. It was a terrible breach of protocol that a copy was ever here."

"So terrible that you broke into my apartment and stole my copies and deleted all my files," Tania protested. "Those copies alone cost me *three hundred and fifty dollars*. Maybe that doesn't mean much to a prince, but that's a lot on a librarian's salary. And I don't even want to think about the hours I put into the *files*. You even deleted the records of my thesis proposal in the University database. The school administration thought I'd had a mental break when I kept insisting that they were there."

"Well, not me *personally*," Rian protested weakly. "It was Small Kingdoms enforcement. I didn't even find out about it until just last month."

Tania's mouth set in an unsympathetic scowl.

"I'll tell you everything I know," Rian promised, feeling her ill regard more keenly than anything that anyone else had ever aimed at him. "I'll make Raval explain magic. I'll show you my dragon. But...I can't do any of that here. Come to Alaska with me. Let me show you."

"Yes," Tania said unexpectedly.

Rian's heart swelled in his chest and his dragon seemed to roar in his ears.

"I won't marry you, and I won't—" Tania cut herself off with a hot blush that said more than her words could. "I won't *whatever*. I need more data, and I want to know all the things that you stole from me."

Rian knew that thirst she was looking at him with. It was exactly the way he felt about her, some combination of physical desire and a desperate need to *know more*. He wanted to sit and have long conversations about things they'd only touched on in emails, he wanted to compare their to-be-read lists, he wanted to tell her all his craziest thoughts, and know hers.

"I'll call Fask and ask him to send the jet," he said, reaching for his phone.

Tania's eyes widened. "Just like that?" She rather suddenly pulled her mouth into a teasing pout. "You aren't going to fly me there on your back the way you came?"

"Could you ride essentially horseback for about ten

hours without a saddle or reins, being buffeted by cold winds high enough in the air that the oxygen is thin?" Rian asked seriously.

Her pout softened thoughtfully. "Ah...no, no I probably could not do that. And no magic portals?"

Rian laughed. "You should ask Raval about magic portals. They're apparently really hard to make, require all kinds of special prep and super high concentration. I don't even get it all, but Raval says it would be like building a nuclear power plant to power a lightbulb instead of just using a flashlight. They're kind of a sore point with him. We used to tease him about them as a kid." Then he thought to ask, "Do you have a passport?"

Tania nodded slowly. "I went to the Caribbean over spring break three years ago. It hasn't expired yet."

Rian desperately wanted to pull her into his arms and kiss her triumphantly. She'd said *yes*. Maybe not yes to *marrying him*, and not to *whatever*, but it was still a *yes*, and *yes* felt like music in his soul.

10

A few days later, Tania could feel her next crash coming. She'd been too wound up to sleep soundly, and the past few days had been non-stop. Packing had been an enormous physical effort, even if Rian hadn't allowed her to carry her luggage once since she left the apartment. He had also promised her to have her books shipped separately, if she decided to stay, but Tania couldn't resist bringing a few of her favorites.

She kept her chin high and her breathing steady, ignoring the ache in her hip, and followed Rian down the stairs to the waiting limo.

She had considered leaving her cane behind, or packing it in her luggage under the plane, but finally wrestled down her pride. She'd be glad of it to lean on while she waited in lines, she thought, or walked the endless length of airport halls. No matter how ugly it was.

To her bemusement, however, there were no lines, and no waiting whatsoever. They were taken in a limo directly to a small, private airfield. Her passport and Rian's were passed through the window, she answered a few stunned questions about agriculture, and they were waved through to park directly at the bottom of a stair up to a waiting private jet sporting a blue tail with gold stars. Probably not real gold.

Uniform or no, it was the first time Tania really appreciated that Rian was an actual *prince*. He was so unassuming, so gentle and kind with her. It was hard to remember that he was in a whole different class.

The airline staff actually bowed to him—to *them*, and the pilot came back to reverently shake their hands and exchange solemn small talk before they took off.

Tania had walked through first class many times in her life, always heading back to the sardine class in the back. This plane didn't even have a sardine class—every single seat in the thing was a leather swivel recliner or an actual couch, all in tasteful white trimmed with probably-not-real gold and white probably-not-real fur. There was a wet bar, and a big screen television facing the couch, and cunning little tables tucked into useful corners. There was even a bookshelf, though it held nothing but magazines.

The mirrored ceiling startled her, until she realized that she was looking up at the reflection of a sky-patterned carpet and her own dazed face. She blushed, thinking of things that might be done under such a thing in a more *private* setting...

Rian politely elbowed a blue-uniformed stewardess out of the way to lead Tania back to a little loveseat next to an enormous window himself. "I hope this will be comfortable," he said, as he tried to figure out the seatbelt in the seat next to her. There was enough space between their loveseat and the chairs opposite to waltz in. "Fask is the one who insists we have the fancy jet. I...ah...don't fly in it much." He triumphed over the buckle.

"Because…" Tania eyed the staff and Rian shook his head discretely. They must not know about certain mythical traits of their own royalty.

A stewardess gave a brief personal safety orientation, and took drink orders—just water for Tania and Rian followed suit. It was brought with a warm cookie, a tiny bowl of warm nuts, and a hot, wet towel.

"Is everything fancier warmed up?" Tania asked Rian in wonder.

"Apparently," Rian said, rolling his eyes in amusement.

Tania even forgot to read her book as they took off, between the distraction of Rian at her side, and the view of Orlando falling away in a tapestry below her, it was not that strangely un-tempting. She clutched at Rian's arm when the plane gave a short lurch and her whole body tensed up in pain, and it seemed perfectly normal to twine her fingers into his and leave them there after that.

She was keenly aware of his closeness, and his attention. The stewardess was kind and professional, but her glance was knowing and full of amusement.

His hand in hers was warm, as was his arm against her. Warm and solid, and he smelled intoxicating, even if Tania couldn't define exactly what it was. Romance books might suggest moss and steel, or whiskey and sandalwood, or some other absurd combination. To Tania's nose, he smelled…safe. She barely kept herself from burying her nose into his shoulder and inhaling, and wondered if she was being improper just by leaning against him.

To her surprise and dismay, she fell asleep on him, not even realizing she was tired until she woke later.

Her intake of breath made Rian stir. "Have a good nap?"

"A mixed blessing," Tania said around her gritted

teeth. Her neck and shoulders protested the uncomfortable position she'd been in, but she did feel more rested.

"My arm is asleep," Rian said, rubbing it cheerfully as Tania cautiously pulled herself upright, braced for the screaming in her joints.

"I'm sorry," she said, in sudden confusion and embarrassment. She'd fallen asleep on a *prince*, she reminded herself. "I didn't mean to do that..."

"There's a bedroom in the back," Rian said kindly. "But I thought that mentioning it would make it sound like I was trying to join the mile-high club. And you didn't say yes to *whatever*."

Tania blushed and couldn't help giggling as she checked her watch. "We probably still have time," she teased, and then she wished she hadn't, because the moment sharpened to a keen intensity and the humor evaporated into charged tension between them.

Her arm felt chilled, now that it wasn't warm against his side, and Tania yearned to lean back into him. His hands flexed, like he was wrestling back the same urge, and Tania wished with all her heart that he would kiss her, the way she was dying to kiss him. They both wanted the same thing...and both of them were too keenly aware that these were orchestrated feelings.

"I should get up and walk around," she said regretfully, when he didn't. "I'm going to be sorry I slept like that."

They unbuckled, and Rian helped Tania to her feet. She was glad she'd decided not to pack the cane under the plane, because even though the flight was smooth and the jet had plenty of space to walk, she was unsteady on her feet. Rian, hovering at her elbow, didn't help with her general dizziness, though she knew he meant well.

He poured her a soda at the wetbar, and she took a mild muscle relaxer from her purse. "I would have woken you, if I'd known," Rian said, frowning. "Do you want to lie down?"

Tania tried to think logically around the fluster in her heart. She ought to be as well-rested as possible when she met Rian's family; she could already feel the hollow nervousness starting to eat at her stomach, and she hadn't slept much the night before. "I'm not feeling tired anymore," she confessed. "But it would probably be a good idea to rest." She hated how weak she sounded, and she wanted to be tougher than she was.

Rian was gently cheerful about it, showing her back to a bed big enough for three or four people covered in a plush white comforter and scattered with fat pillows.

She crawled onto it, feeling terrifically self-conscious. Rian fluffed a few of the pillows, rescuing one from the floor, and fussed kindly over her as she managed to upend her purse. Her unread book fell out and he picked it up for her.

"Want me to read to you?" he offered with a grin.

Tania hesitated; she had just been regretting that the most comfortable position she could find wasn't going to allow her to hold a book or tablet. "I'm not sure you want to read that book to me," she said frankly, blushing.

"Time traveling romance is my favorite," Rian deadpanned. "I've been thinking about getting a kilt of my own." He opened the book absolutely shamelessly and settled into the chair next to the bed. "'It was a dark and stormy night...'" he started dramatically.

Tania let herself settle comfortably back into the fluffy pillows. "I'm pretty sure that's not how it starts."

Then he started reading in earnest, and Tania let herself close her eyes and just listen.

His voice was utterly beautiful, he read smoothly, and

he even did a Scottish accent that grew more confident as he went along.

She didn't sleep, too caught up in Rian's reading; he had a gorgeous voice that gave her shivers to her toes. He didn't even hesitate over the ridiculously intimate bits, and he lingered lovingly over the lush descriptions, even when Tania had to stifle her giggles in one of the pillows.

Listening to him talk about clever fingers and kisses was a fabulous new distraction, and Tania found herself remembering that she was lying on a bed...a wide bed with plenty of room for—

A throat clearing at the doorway made her eyes fly open and the stewardess blushed. "Sorry to interrupt," she said apologetically. "I have a choice of chicken parmesan, or sausage-stuffed shells for your dinner."

"I love both of those," Tania said in delighted surprise.

The stewardess exchanged an amused look with Rian. "They were at his highness' request," she explained.

"You used to rave about that Italian place two blocks away," Rian reminded her. "I got them to put a couple of orders together since I didn't know which you liked better. There's a kitchen, so they'll be fresh baked."

Tania had almost forgotten they were flying. She had certainly forgotten that she had ever mentioned a favorite restaurant. It must have been one of their earliest email exchanges. "This is amazing," she said, shaking her head. "The shells, please."

"The other one is fine for me," Rian said.

The stewardess vanished, grinning.

"You want to take a shower first?" Rian offered.

"Now you're just pulling my leg," Tania said skeptically.

"There's no bathtub, sorry," Rian said, with exaggerated apology.

But there really *was* a shower, and after a moment of reluctance, Tania decided that if she wasn't going to indulge herself now, in a fancy jet winging its way thousands of miles from her home, she never was. Her carry-on was already in the bedroom, tucked away in a clever closet, and Rian grinned and latched the bedroom door behind him as he left.

11

*R*ian was reluctant to walk away from her and shut the bedroom door. Every step away felt wrong, and he had to pace the length of the plane several times until he was calm enough to sit and try to read the book that he'd brought.

It was quite a bit less gripping than the ridiculous kilted fluff he'd been reading to Tania, and he was constantly distracted by his imagination supplying the reminder that she was naked, wet, and soapy, and not so very far away. The muffled hum of the jet engines drowned out any sounds of the shower.

He was happy to put the volume aside when she emerged from the bedroom with her cheeks flushed and her hair damp around her shoulders.

She was leaning less heavily on her cane, Rian thought. Should he offer to dry her hair? She had once mentioned in an email that it was a hassle to care for it and she'd been considering cutting it; he had protested, but now that he understood a little better what she was going through, he felt like he'd been insensitive.

"How was your shower?" he asked neutrally.

"Decadent," Tania said, as she sank down opposite from him. "It was hot and the pressure was good, and it had more handholds than any shower I've ever seen."

"In case of turbulence," Rian said, smiling foolishly across the table.

"It's insane that I'm on a plane," Tania said, looking out the bright window over the clouds. "Is it much further?"

"A few hours," Rian confirmed, looking at his watch.

The stewardess brought a tray of hot towels and spread napkins in their laps, then served a fresh, delicious dinner.

"How long does it take when you…" Tania glanced at the stewardess, who was out of earshot brewing a pot of coffee. "Fly solo?"

"A little longer, about ten hours."

Tania tsked disapprovingly. "Not as fast as a jet plane, hmm?"

Rian laughed.

"How do you keep people from seeing you?" Tania asked, one eye on the stewardess across the plane as she gracefully ate.

"It's a natural defense. Anyone looking up will see a shimmer of light at the most, maybe a hint of a sun dog. It looks like northern lights at night."

Tania's eyes got round. "I've never seen the northern lights. Oh my gosh, will I get to? I should have packed a Dana Stabenow."

"It's the right time of year," Rian said, grinning at her enthusiasm. "You have a good chance."

The stewardess took their dishes and brought them hot towels and more warm cookies. Rian gave his second cookie to Tania, because it was more fun to watch her eat them and lick melted chocolate from her fingers than it was to eat them himself.

They went back to the couch and buckled up again at the stewardess' not-really-a-suggestion. "Do you want me to read to you again?" Rian offered awkwardly. He wanted to take her hand, but didn't.

Tania blushed and smiled. "No, you've served your time, I'll finish the book myself."

Rian opened his own book, but he found himself drawn to looking over it most of the rest of the flight. Outside the windows, fluffy clouds in deepening colors streamed along below them, and Tania watched them while Rian watched her and tried to analyze the ache he was feeling. Her pain? His longing?

She was a fighter, Rian thought. Not the same kind of in-your-face, you-can't-make-me, take-on-the-establishment fighter as Carina, but Tania still picked her battles and saw them through. She hadn't given up on her thesis even when it was made literally impossible. She still fought for a life of dignity and independence as her body tried to fail her.

He pulled out a tablet and made a few notes about his earlier reading, then returned to his book.

She didn't fall asleep on him again, to Rian's faint disappointment, and they had both made solid inroads on their literature by the time they finally landed, smoothly, in Fairbanks. It was already dark, and Tania craned to see the sky, probably hopeful for auroras.

The stewardess brought Tania a big coat with a fur ruff, which she bemusedly put on. "It's not that cold yet," Rian told her. "But your Florida jacket won't be enough."

Tania, stepping out onto the stairway, shivered and cuddled deeper into the coat. "Not that cold *yet*, you say? What have I *done?*"

Rian's glasses promptly fogged up in the cold air and he took them off to tuck into a coat pocket.

To Rian's surprise, they were met at the bottom of the stairs by a full honor guard, led by Captain Luke herself, and escorted swiftly to a waiting cavalcade. Rian shot the captain a curious look and stepped aside while Tania was helped into the limo; usually royal arrivals were met with one or two guards and one car, and Luke was rarely part of such an informal greeting.

"There's been an incident," Luke said in a low growl. If she was surprised that Tania walked slowly and used a cane, she was too polite to show it. Rian had warned his brothers, but he wasn't sure how much they had prepared the rest of the staff.

"Princess Carina?" They had all started calling her princess since the engagement party, though she wouldn't technically be one until the wedding, planned for early the following month.

Captain Luke gave a crisp nod, but didn't offer to explain. She got into the passenger seat next to the driver of his limo after she closed his door.

The limo was too wide to give Rian an excuse to cuddle close to Tania, so he satisfied himself by looking out the window and pointing out some of the sights in the faint light that remained. "There's a view of the mountain, Denali, that way during the day. The name means Great One in the Native language, and it's appropriate. Did you know, you wouldn't be able to see it from here due to the curvature of the earth if it weren't for the atmosphere bending the light?"

"I didn't know that," Tania said. "I can't wait to see it."

"I hope it's clear tomorrow," Rian said sincerely.

"It's so weird," Tania said. "My body thinks it's eleven

at night, but it's only seven here...but the light suggests late at night like the rest of me."

"It gets dark early, this time of the year. In the summer, we never get darker than civil twilight, for several months. In winter, it's the opposite, we only get a few hours of daylight."

"How do you get anything done?" Tania wanted to know. "I'd never want to get out of bed if it was always dark." She bit her lip and looked away quickly, and Rian wanted to believe that she was thinking about a bed with *company*, the way he was. He couldn't help it. Between his dragon, who kept insisting that *she was the one*, the simple beauty of her, and the way he was already half in love with her, he was having the worst time keeping his thoughts from straying.

"We have this amazing invention known as the electric light," he teased, and was rewarded by her quick smile and laugh. "It's almost like magic!"

Tania laughed and socked him gently in the arm. She didn't seem to think there was anything unusual in their nervous guard. Rian didn't want to alarm her, so he didn't tell her about Luke's news, but it certainly alarmed him.

Alaska was a rich country, rich in both land and resources, and he knew that relations with some of the other Small Kingdoms nations were strained, even if he didn't follow politics closely. There were many who would like to see the country fail to attend the Renewal, the centennial gathering that reset the Compact and refreshed the spell. Alaska needed a king to send. If they could not, they would be cut out of the Compact entirely, and lose all of the protections that kept their enemies from acting.

The Renewal required a king's attendance. And a king was selected by finding his mate. Rian studied Tania's profile and wondered if he'd done her any favors. If he'd put her in danger…

"Oh!" she said. "Oh, it's beautiful!"

Rian looked at the castle he'd been born in with fresh eyes. He'd always felt like it was too modern, trying too hard to be relevant. It was a mash-up of grand and modest, rustic and luxurious. It mimicked some of the aesthetic of mountain lodges, but managed somehow to be more intimidating. There were broad balconies, perfect for landing on as a dragon, and it was a mix of stone and solid log.

This time of year, it was lit all over with lights, in all colors, that reflected off the snow. The evergreens that ringed the drive were all heavy with fresh snow, and it looked like a winter paradise.

Tania's hand brushed his as she leaned across the seat to gawk up at the towers as the driver pulled them up to the front doors. Already, guards were boiling out of the building; more guards than Rian was used to seeing.

The door was opened for him, and he turned to help Tania out and let her catch her balance before walking up the broad steps, not allowing Luke hurry them.

He was surprised and delighted when Tania slipped her hand into his.

12

*E*verything felt just slightly surreal.

Tania had seen photographs of the Alaska royal castle, but somehow, they didn't do justice to the looming greatness of the structure, or the quirky elegance of it. Part cabin, part castle, it was somehow in perfect balance.

She put her hand in Rian's without thinking about it, and only when he squeezed her fingers did she consider that it might give the wrong impression. She hadn't said *yes* to anything but coming to Alaska and learning more. Maybe she was implying more than she wanted to, even if it wasn't more than she actually wanted...

She didn't want to pull her hand free, both because she didn't want to embarrass him or confuse matters further, and because his touch made her feel so safe.

Once they were inside, they were greeted by a small party. Tania recognized Fask, the oldest brother, at once, and he stepped forward to greet her, making all the perfect conversation and introductions. He had the air of *someone important*, as Rian didn't. He knew his own consequence, and was clearly willing to take command. Everything about him suggested *king*. He even had a dark, neatly-trimmed beard to complete the image.

She had to take her hand from Rian's to shake Fask's, because her other hand was holding her cane, and it left her feeling adrift. "Tania," she introduced herself. "Tania Perez."

"You may call me Fask," he said warmly.

"Thank you," Tania said, hoping it was the correct response.

Toren came eagerly to take her hand next, and then Carina, who looked at her with great relief and took her hand in both of hers for a warm squeeze-and-shake. Carina was lithe and athletic, and she bounced a little on her feet as she told Tania to make herself completely at home.

"We've been traveling a long while," Rian reminded everyone firmly, and although Tania wanted to protest that flying in a fancy jet with a shower couldn't be considered a hardship, it felt very late, and she was honestly exhausted.

When everyone looked at her, she admitted, "I'm a bit out of spoons."

They all looked puzzled and Tania knew she'd been too obscure. Just as she wondered if she should explain the concept, Fask quickly said, "Of course! Rian? Mrs. James has prepared the Sage Suite for her."

"I'll show you where it is," Rian said at once, and then his hand was in hers like it belonged there and everyone was grinning at them with annoying amusement.

"Can you do the stairs?" he asked her quietly as Tania looked around for her luggage and found it already being carried by a pair of solemn-faced guards who were clearly prepared to follow them. She had a pang of guilt for the weight of her books. "We've got an elevator, but it's at the other end of the west wing and kind of a hike."

"I can do the stairs," Tania said firmly. She could right now, anyway.

She stepped as briskly as she could, her cane only for balance, and they came to a large second floor landing just as her hip reminded her that pride came before a fall, sometimes literally in her case. To the left opened a great, dark hall, hinting at echoing empty space. To the right was a hallway, and it felt smaller and homey, with double doors in slight alcoves, like a fancy hotel. Rian took her to one about halfway to the end, and opened it for her.

It was not just a room, but a suite of rooms, beautifully appointed in warm golden wood, with sage-green plush carpeting and walls just a shade lighter. The modest bedroom was through a doorway, a bed made with a warm comforter folded down to reveal pure white sheets. A warm lamp beside the bed was the only lighting on in that room, and Tania thought it looked like the coziest thing she'd ever seen. The living area was appointed with brown leather furniture, and Tania thought that the only thing missing to make it a perfect living room were bookshelves.

A gleaming bathroom was nestled by the bedroom door, white marble, from Tania's glance, with dark green towels.

It was, in whole, about three times the size of her entire apartment.

"It's beautiful," she said. "Thank you so much."

Rian looked like he was trying to decide how far in it would be polite to come, and he very carefully did not look towards the bedroom. The two guards were not so restrained, carrying her bags with professional neutrality directly in, leaving them on waiting luggage racks, and bowing before they left the room. To her surprise, they did not go far, but settled obviously on either side of the door.

"I'm just upstairs if you need anything," Rian said, looking uncharacteristically nervous. "Up the stairs and to the right. Just above this room. Exactly above it. You can't miss it."

He was still holding her hand, and Tania wondered who was clinging to whom. She desperately wanted him to stay and he seemed to have no desire to leave.

"Tania," he said quietly. "If there's anything you need..."

There was *so much* that she needed. She needed his touch, she needed his kiss, with an intensity that frightened her. She needed to drag him back to that big, beautiful bed and pull him down with her at last, to give herself over to this crazy fairy tale fantasy that she'd found herself in.

"I can't think of anything," she lied politely.

He let go of her hand at last, but didn't draw any further away. "Breakfast will be at nine," he said gruffly. "In the informal dining room. It's on this floor, just left of the stairs. You'll see it."

"Oh, just the *informal* dining room," Tania said in wonder, giving a hiccup of a laugh as she looked up at him.

Rian smiled at her, quick and crooked, then dipped towards her impulsively and gave her a swift kiss on the forehead. "Sleep well," he said.

"Sweet dreams," she whispered in reply.

She stood where she was as he left with a quick, casual bow, and closed the double doors behind him.

She swayed in place for a moment, then wearily went to unpack and fall into her gorgeous bed, in a gorgeous castle, and dream of her gorgeous prince.

13

Rian stood in front of Tania's room for a long moment, straining to hear her in case she called him back. He remembered the guards only after too much time had passed to pretend he was doing anything else, and scowled at them in embarrassment. They continued to look woodenly across the hall and Rian swiftly went back out of the wing, to the big receiving room overlooking the woods and mountains to the south. Toren, Carina, and Fask were waiting there.

Rian had chickened out of calling Fask on the phone and put it all in an email; he was bringing home the Compact scholar, and she was his mate. Presumably he had told the rest of the family the news, by now. He didn't look particularly happy.

They will know each other, his dragon murmured in satisfaction.

Rian caught a flash of understanding in Toren's face.

"She seems lovely," Fask said blandly.

"She is," Rian said as mildly as he could manage in

return. "What happened to Carina? Where are Raval and Tray? Is *Tania* in danger here?"

"Raval and Tray are patrolling the area," Fask said. Not only did dragons have the advantage over humans of being able to fly, they were also more sensitive to magic and could pick up any traces of it that lingered after a spell.

"Someone triggered the back perimeter alarm," Toren explained. Rian still wasn't used to him taking part in anything more serious than a discussion about hockey scores. "And then they got into the vault. Raval was down there and he was able to stop them."

Rian frowned. "Wait, you said they activated the back perimeter. How did they get from there to the vault? And why would you assume this was an attempt on Carina if they were going for the vault?"

"Raval was there; they came in through a portal," Fask said grimly. "They left a half-burnt page at the scene. At least part of it was the portal spell, used up, and part of the rest referenced a mate. Raval wants more time to make sense of it, but there wasn't much left. Your jet hadn't even taken off when it happened, so it seems unlikely that Tania was the target."

Toren had one fist in a ball at his side, his other arm firmly around Carina.

"A portal?" Rian said, alarmed by several parts of the statement. "Who has the power to do portals?"

Equally grim expressions answered him. "Raval thinks it was a one-time gambit," Fask said, his tone more reassuring than his face. "That kind of thing was an all-or-nothing, no one could do multiple incursions like that."

"And they *got* nothing," Toren said with satisfaction.

Incursions. Rian didn't like the sound of it. There had been occasional periods of time growing up when things were tense and there were extra guards on guests, but no one had *ever* broken through the perimeters. And portals were like nuclear weapons; he knew that they existed in theory, but he never expected anyone to use one. Not against them.

"Why the vault?" Rian asked. "If they were after Carina, why would they end up there? What did Raval do?"

"Raval said he caught a woman trying to get the pages of the Compact out of the case. He grabbed one of Father's swords, and drove her back into the portal. He said it was dark on the other side, and there was an explosion before the portal closed," Toren explained.

Fask paced thoughtfully along the window looking out over the front drive. "It's possible that the Compact protections redirected it. If this was an act of one of the Small Kingdoms against us, their spell may have been diverted to a place it could do no damage to us. Raval said that the chance of him being there at that moment to intercept the portal was impossibly slim; he thinks that there's a *reason* it happened. And if they were testing the protections of the Compact...probably they learned their lesson."

Rian felt ruffled. Even if the Compact had done exactly what it should and guarded them, the fact that they'd been targeted was unnerving. He wasn't worried for himself, but if Tania was in any danger...

"Are you sure that Tania is your mate?" Fask might have been following his train of thought.

"There's no doubt," Rian said confidently.

"And Carina is still your mate?" Fask asked Toren and Carina.

Toren gave him a crooked grin. "My dragon hasn't changed his tune. Honestly, Fask, there's no lying about that kind of thing. It's not like you could pretend, and just show up at the Renewal, and fool the *Compact*. What would be the point?"

"So, why are there two of them?" Fask wanted to know.

"The Compact has a sense of humor?" Toren suggested.

"Raval was investigating whether or not we could somehow deliberately activate a mate for Fask instead," Rian reminded them. "That's the whole reason I ended up finding Tania, remember. Maybe the act of the investigation itself triggered something?"

Fask frowned. "Raval said he couldn't make sense of those parts of the Compact. And this doesn't match anything we know. The most obvious reasons I can think of a second mate activating...aren't pleasant." He glanced at Toren.

Toren's face went pale and Carina bit her lip. "You think...?"

"The Compact is supposed to provide a mate when it is *needed,*" Fask said gravely. "If we lost Carina..."

"Maybe it's a delayed reaction," Rian said. "Someone tried to kill Carina a few weeks ago. Maybe the Compact activated a second mate at that time, and now we just get two."

"You think Carina was *supposed* to *die* then? Because Drayger wasn't actually trying to kill her. He defected, remember?" Toren looked very young and uncertain again, not at all like the crown prince he'd been trying to be.

"Drayger wasn't trying to kill her, but Shadow was. Or AmCo Bank was, and he was their assassin. He had fooled everyone here into thinking he was a dog, so there were plenty of opportunities for him to succeed. AmCo isn't in the Small Kingdoms; the Compact wouldn't be able to protect her. Predicting the future is...complicated. Maybe it's only looking at *possible* futures. If Carina's death was a high possibility, maybe that...triggered something."

"That's not at *all* unnerving," Carina said, clearly trying to sound flippant but only managing to sound afraid.

Fask heaved a great sigh. "The Compact also doesn't offer protection from physical attack, only magical. I don't want Carina or Tania to leave the grounds for now."

"The wedding?" Toren asked.

"We're clearing and warding Angel Hot Springs right now. Captain Luke has approved it, with precautions. She'd rather have extra people there than here. It won't be the largest wedding we've hosted, we're keeping it small and intimate. And speaking of weddings…" Fask turned his gaze to Rian.

"Tania hasn't said yes," he said reluctantly.

"She's your mate," Fask pointed out.

"That doesn't mean I can force her to marry me," Rian said defensively. "Or that I'd *want* to force her."

"Rian's older than me," Toren said abruptly. "If he does marry Tania, that means he's the king, right? I mean, I was just on the hook because I was the only one with a mate?"

"She hasn't said yes," Rian repeated.

"Did you ask her?" Carina asked with a chuckle.

"Yes," Rian said flatly. She hadn't said yes to marrying him...or yes to *whatever*.

"I want to know more about her," Fask said gravely. "You said she was a librarian? That she was studying the secret version of the Compact? How did she get it?"

"The public library in Orlando had it on microfiche," Rian said. "She first did a report on it for a high school history class and later turned it into a thesis when she went on to college."

"Microwhat?" Toren wanted to know.

"They used to photograph old documents and periodicals and store them on rolls of film before everything went digital. Brutal way to do research because all the indexing had to be done manually," Rian explained briefly.

Toren looked unimpressed.

"How would the microfiche even get there?" Fask asked.

Rian bit back his frustration and pushed his glasses up on his nose. "How would I know? The Compact works in mysterious ways?"

"We should have a meeting tomorrow," Fask said patiently. "We'll work out who might be behind the breach and what they might want. I'll ask Drayger if he's heard anything. Rian, you look beat. It's late, we'll hit this again tomorrow."

"Welcome home," Toren said wryly.

Rian realized that he was pretty well dead on his feet. Was that all his own exhaustion, or was he feeling Tania's? "Thanks," he said sincerely. "It's a little colder than Florida, and it was a long flight."

He shook hands with Fask again, Carina gave him an impulsive hug, and he and Toren exchanged a brief embrace.

Toren and Carina went giggling down the hallway as Rian paused at the bottom of the stairs up to the third floor. He desperately wanted to return to Tania's rooms. The guards wouldn't stop him. He sighed and started up the broad steps.

She hadn't said yes to 'whatever.'

14

Tania woke up feeling better than she had in...maybe years.

Part of it was the bed—Tania stretched carefully and could not reach edge to edge with her hands. It was also probably the nicest mattress she had ever slept on, and the room was pleasantly cool and almost eerily silent. There were no city noises, no neighbors shouting or dogs barking.

Part of it was that she had been through a long exciting day of travel and she'd taken a muscle relaxer to make sure she didn't suffer too badly for it. She looked at her phone for the time without turning it on. She should have a chance to take a quick shower before breakfast if she didn't tarry, and her stomach grumbled at the thought of food.

The view out her windows was extraordinary. There was a pink sky of early pre-sunrise that made Tania double-check her phone for the time again, spread out over a forest of Christmas trees frosted in snow. There was a curious blue cast over everything, and white mountains were just visible against the skyline. As she watched, a pair of ravens twisted overhead and disappeared into the forest. She left the window reluctantly to pad to the bathroom.

Hot water spilled from a rain head, and it took all of Tania's willpower to get out of the shower after she had finished sampling the range of soaps and shampoos.

Only food—and the thought of finding Rian again—drove Tania out of the blissful water and into a nearly-as-blissful towel, thick and soft. She dried her hair and scowled at the badly grown-out highlights and unruly bangs, then sighed and got dressed.

Her guards were still there, waiting outside her door. The same ones? she wondered, as they turned attentively when she cracked the door open.

"I was planning on, um, breakfast," she said, pointing, as if they might not know the direction to the dining room. The *informal* dining room.

"Very good," one of them grumbled. The other gave a brief smile.

Tania was still too timid to ask their names, and it was very weird indeed to walk out into the hallway and have them follow her.

At the end of the hall, before it opened into the top of the stairwell, a figure suddenly appeared, and it took Tania a moment to figure out why he was so strange, and why she was so alarmed when he reached out his hand to take hers.

She stepped back, instead.

"Did I deceive you?" he asked with a boyish grin.

Tania had to look hard at him. "No," she said honestly. "I knew you weren't Rian. But you do look very much like him."

"Not even a little bit of doubt?" Tray—for that's who it had to be—asked with disappointment. He took the glasses he'd been wearing off and tucked them into a pocket.

"Not for a second," Tania said with a chuckle. "But I

did already know he had an identical twin, so maybe that's why I wasn't fooled."

"Well, I'll show you to the dining room," Tray said, and this time Tania did let him tuck her hand into his elbow. "Welcome to our home, I'm sorry I didn't get a chance to greet you properly last night."

It was still much darker outside than Tania expected for nine in the morning; the October sky was still rosy and the sun seemed to be tangled in the trees outside the sweeping windows to the south; she'd never seen such a slow sunrise.

"Oh, look," Tray teased. "It's my twin brother, Tray."

Rian, sitting at the table, looked outraged, but Tania chuckled nervously. "He didn't fool me," she promised, and she nearly went to kiss him, it felt so natural, then remembered that she hadn't said *yes* to that and wasn't at all sure what to do.

Everyone seemed to be staring at her.

Rian glared at Tray and pulled the chair next to him out. "Here, Tania. You've clearly met Tray, this is Raval."

Raval was the only blonde of the brothers, and he had eyes that were more blue than silver. "Nice to meet you," he said politely, nodding from across the table.

Fask was sitting past Rian at the end of the table, though a chair was conspicuously empty at the head. Carina and Toren sat opposite from him, and nodded politely in greeting. Carina gave a brief, excited wave and a big, friendly smile. The meal seemed curiously casual, with plates piled high with pancakes and bacon being passed back and forth as the brothers teased each other.

"Did you have a nice night?" Fask asked. "I hope you were comfortable."

"Oh, yes, thank you," Tania said politely, serving herself a modest plate of food. She was surprisingly hungry, and the offerings were tempting. There were a plethora of syrups, berry sauces, fresh fruit and whipped cream to top the pancakes with.

"Mrs. James would like to consult with you this afternoon about the engagement announcement and arrangements," Fask told her. "There may be enough time to coordinate it as a double wedding, otherwise we'll need to consider how closely we want to stack events."

Tania had just taken a heaping bite of berries and tart sourdough pancake, and it went dry in her mouth. "Oh, I..." she tried to say around it, reaching for her water. She felt a moment of panic and excitement, sheer adrenaline choking her.

"We're not engaged," Rian said, swallowing more quickly than she could. "We're not planning *anything* yet."

Tania coughed on the water she was trying to drink, and Carina laughed sympathetically, and then swiftly sobered when Tania didn't join her in mirth. "It took Toren a long time to remember to actually ask me to marry him," she said kindly. "There were a lot of assumptions made."

Tania exchanged a helpless look with Rian, who growled, "She hasn't said yes." He quickly added, "And she doesn't have to!" and glared around the table daring anyone to disagree.

His statement was met with varying levels of dubiousness and surprise. Tray said in a stage whisper to Raval, "She's holding out for an upgrade to the superior twin."

That elicited some giggles, and even Tania chuckled a little as she took another tentative bite of her food. The bacon was the perfect balance of crispy and chewy, and deliciously smoky. No one pushed further on the topic of their future, but Tania had the feeling that she and Rian were the only ones in the room who weren't certain that it was already written in stone.

As breakfast was cleared away, Tania found herself evaluating her state and was pleasantly surprised to find that she was not in terrible shape. The journey hadn't been that grueling, and her sleep had been restful. The bed had certainly been magnificent.

"Do you want to come see Phoebe's puppies?" Tray offered, just as Tania was wondering what happened next.

"Oh, they are so cute," Carina encouraged her. "They're getting to a really fun age, too, you should definitely come and see them with us!"

Tania glanced at Rian, and Fask frowned thoughtfully at them. "Rian, I'd like to speak with you." Tania's exclusion was clear and she wasn't sure if she felt relieved or slighted. Mostly the former, she decided.

Toren laughed. "You're going to get *the talk*," he predicted. "Kingly this and royal that…" Tania thought that the expression on his face was relief; he clearly thought that Rian would be taking the title of crown prince from him and he was glad of it. But if Rian was crown prince…that would make *her*— "I'd love to meet the puppies," she said quickly.

Tray led Carina and Tania through the back of the castle to a cool, concrete-floored room that felt like a garage, but was laid out with several battered couches and chewed-up chairs. In one corner was a play pen with an open crate.

"This is Phoebe, and her pups," Tray said, as proudly as if he'd had the puppies himself.

"Aren't they darling?" Carina said in delight, her voice a full octave higher than it had been. "They're three weeks old now, and we're going to be naming them soon."

Phoebe, a black and white dog with upright ears and a

tail that was thumping in delight against the crate, looked up and whined in greeting. Four squirming puppies were staggering around beside her, investigating the folds in the blanket and the corners of the pen. They ranged in color from fawn to black, with the same cape-and-mask markings as their mother, but much muddier.

And they really were the cutest things Tania had probably ever seen, clumsy and fuzzy and full of squeaks as they tried to attack each other and generally fell on their faces. Their ears were still flopped over adorably.

"This one is mine," Carina said, kneeling beside the crate to scoop up one of the bigger ones with chocolate markings. "I'm thinking about calling her Moose."

Maybe-Moose had a tiny pink tongue, and she tried to lick Carina furiously, whining and wiggling in her arms.

"Oh, she's cute," Tania agreed, using her cane to kneel beside her. When she tried to pet the tiny thing, it growled and gnawed harmlessly on her finger, then licked wildly and nearly squirmed from Carina's arms. "How fierce!"

"This one's probably more your speed," Tray said as he picked up a quieter puppy with pale markings. Then he looked mortified, like he suspected he'd insulted her.

Tania smiled reassuringly and set her cane aside so she could gather the puppy into her arms.

The puppy immediately tried—and failed—to climb up to Tania's face, pawing helplessly as she toppled to one side and ended up on her back. Tania easily caught her and cuddled her close. The puppy seemed content to gnaw on her finger and accept pets rather than trying to wriggle free again—unlike Maybe-Moose, who was desperately trying to escape Carina's affections and return to her brothers, who were wrestling and growling.

"Oh my gosh, she is so darling!" Tania caught herself

going up an octave like Carina had. Even Tray was cooing at the boys as he sat and stroked Phoebe.

"You want a dog?" Tray offered. "She likes you!"

Tania looked at him in alarm.

"It's kind of an Alaska thing," Carina laughed, winding the squirmy Maybe-Moose back into her arms. "Welcome to the monarchy. Here's your starter dog."

Tania had stopped petting the furry, amorphous little sausage and it whined and wiggled and licked until she resumed. "I don't need a dog," she protested weakly, already half in love with the creature. "I'm...more of a cat person."

"Do you have any cats, back in Florida?" Carina looked completely innocent, but Tania could see that she was dying to pry more into Tania's background.

"No," Tania said. "Most of the college housing wouldn't accept pets. I thought about sneaking one in, but never did." And then she hadn't had the energy for a pet.

"Lawful good," Carina theorized.

"Too chicken to jeopardize my scholarship," Tania countered. Of course, the scholarship had run out with her thesis.

Carina grinned at her. "I hear you! But just look how much she likes you!"

The puppy was wiggling and whining more urgently now, and Tania had to put more attention into keeping her from tumbling out of her embrace altogether.

"Oh, wait—" Tray warned too late.

The puppy gave a little yip of dismay and peed down the front of Tania's shirt. Tania felt her face heat in dismay.

"Sorry," Tray said. "She's still just a baby."

"I probably should have realized," Tania said, putting her down on the puppy pad in their pen. Carina put

Maybe-Moose down just in time to do her business in the right place. One of her brothers managed to stagger directly into the stream of pee and get a soaked paw, which made him yelp in protest and faceplant trying to shake it off.

"Well," Tania said, dabbing at her shirt with a towel that Tray sheepishly provided, "I guess she's really claimed me for her own." She tried to laugh and looked up to their hopeful expressions, wondering if she had missed a beat for humor. "Because canines pee on things to claim them?" Jokes were never funny if you had to explain them, and she felt ridiculously stupid until Tray began to grin.

"I won't tell Nathan you said that," he chortled.

Carina was giggling, too, and Tania looked in puzzlement between them. "Who is Nathan?"

Carina was quick to explain, "He's the groundskeeper, and he helps with the dog yards."

Tania still wasn't sure where the joke was until Tray added, "He's a wolf shifter."

"A...*wolf* shifter?" Tania knew she looked foolish. She certainly *felt* foolish. Shouldn't someone who might be the next queen of Alaska already know these things? "Like a werewolf? I...didn't know there *were* other kinds of shifters. Just...dragons..."

Carina and Tray exchanged a look, and they all stood up in unspoken agreement, Tania using her cane to get her to her feet.

"It's kind of crazy," Carina said sympathetically. "All these amazing magical things. There are all kinds of normal secret animal shifters, they aren't all dragons. Captain Luke is a polar bear."

Tania gave a dry chuckle. "I don't even know what questions to ask," she confessed. "Every time I think I have a handle on all the things I don't know, there's something completely out of left field."

"I know what you mean," Carina said sympathetically. "There's a lot to learn, and get caught up on, but we'll all help you. Don't hesitate to ask. When you figure out the questions."

She smiled winningly, and Tania could not help smiling back. "I think I'll go shower and change my shirt, if you don't mind," she said. "Dog pee is not my best look, and it's a terrible perfume." It was also uncomfortably *damp*.

"Of course!" Carina said as the two women walked up a set of shallow concrete steps back into the polished castle. Tray stayed behind with the dogs, and two pairs of guards fell into step a respectful distance behind them. "Hey, if there's anything you need, all you have to do is ask. They're not letting us go anywhere, but we could schedule an appointment with the hairdresser to come here, if you want, and nails, maybe a massage. And we can order any clothes you might need."

Tania gave her a swift sideways look and decided that it wasn't a dig on her untidy hair and unrefined clothing, that Carina was genuinely just trying to be friendly.

Carina confirmed it with a shy smile. "I feel kind of weird asking someone to come to the castle just for myself, but if you wanted a little pampering, too..."

"I'd like that," Tania said gratefully.

Carina drew up. They were at the bottom of the back stairs, Tania realized from her study of the layout, and her rooms were up one flight. "This is all really weird and crazy, I should know, and if you ever need anything, just let me know, okay? I've been where you are, and it's all a little nuts and overwhelming, and these guys, bless their big dragon hearts, have no idea."

Tania had to laugh, swaying on her cane for balance.

"Alright," she promised. "I will. And I really *could* use a haircut, and maybe a color?" She brushed back her bangs in demonstration.

"I'll get Mrs. James right on it!" Carina promised joyfully.

Then, with more energy than Tania could even imagine having, she bounded away on the first floor, leaving Tania to take the stairs up to her suite. Two of the guards peeled off after her.

Carina had probably been under even more pressure than Tania was, she thought wryly, since she had been the One True Hope until Tania showed up. The succession was now somewhat muddled, which was stressful, but probably not as stressful as what Carina had faced. Maybe they were supposed to co-rule? Tania found herself climbing slower as she considered some of the tangled legal language of the Compact. It was easier to think about that in an abstract fashion, far easier than thinking about herself as a queen.

She glanced back once, and wondered if the guards resented being assigned to such a slowpoke. They were shuffling diplomatically behind her, faces blank.

She nearly walked into an old woman waiting at the corner near her room. "I'm sorry," she said, pausing to steady herself again.

"Sometimes, broken things are stronger," the woman said.

Tania glanced back to see if her guards were alarmed, but they both looked perfectly neutral, and not the slightest bit helpful. When she looked back, the old woman had vanished. Was she Mrs. James? Tania wondered. She'd been told about the housekeeper, but not introduced yet. After a moment, she continued on to her rooms, where she changed her clothes and was dismayed to find a flurry of messages on her phone. She had known her trip wouldn't be kept a secret...but she'd hoped.

Her mother's recordings varied between shock (you're marrying a foreign prince?! It's all over the news!), accusation (are you avoiding your mother because you don't want her to have any part of your newfound riches? Did you think it would stay a secret?), heavy-handed guilt (after all I've done for you! The sacrifices I've made!), and complaining about how clearly Tania didn't care a jot for her mother's needs and comforts.

Tania listened to each of her mother's tirades, and decided that was as much energy as she needed to expend for the moment. She would call her back in the morning, when she had spent some time bracing for a one-sided conversation.

Was Rian still meeting with Fask? she wondered. His rooms were right above hers, so she knew basically how to find him; would it be terribly forward of her to show up at his door?

For a moment she was conflicted; it would be very pleasant to simply hide in her rooms and read a book. But there was a part of her that thought it would be even better to enjoy her book in Rian's company. She couldn't explain how much safer she felt near him. *Magic*, she reminded herself.

She sucked in her breath and all the courage she could muster, left her phone, took her book, and braved the judgement of the guards. They trailed her slowly up the steep, endless staircase to the third floor, and she regretted that the elevator was on the opposite end of the castle.

15

"I think I've been adopted by a dog," Tania greeted Rian, to his great surprise. Then her jaw dropped. "Oh. Oh…"

She gazed past him in utter awe and Rian stepped aside to let her walk in, watching as her face lit up.

"You didn't tell me you *lived* in a library!"

The two-story walls of Rian's suite were lined with bookcases, floor to ceiling, end to end. Only windows broke the columns of books, draped in heavy cream-colored velvet to shut out the endless sun on summer nights, and to mask the winter darkness. Floor lamps and comfortable chairs were scattered companionably around, and the door to the bedroom was open, showing the fact that the bookcases continued there…and that he hadn't made his bed.

Rian winced, but it was too late to shut the door or throw the comforter over. Tania looked swiftly past it, flushed, and wandered further into the room. "You have a card catalog?" she squeaked in sudden delight.

"I found it at auction," Rian said. "It cost more to ship

it up here than I paid for it. No cards, so I just use it as an end table. And for storage. Extra buttons, and such. In case I need one to pawn for dinner."

Tania smiled and trailed her fingers over the stained wood. "They had already moved to digital by the time I got my library card," she said longingly. "But they had one of these on display. I love the idea of them."

She was clutching a book and her whole face was lit up.

"Did you…ah…need something?" Rian asked. "If there's anything…" *Whatever,* he thought achingly.

"Oh no," she said swiftly. "I just…" she flushed. "I just thought I'd come read with you."

Rian's heart gave a little lurch in his chest. "You are so the girl for me," he laughed. "The Compact could not have picked anyone better in the world."

He didn't realize he was staring at her until she looked away, and her eyes fell on the newspaper he'd been reading.

"Wait, *what?*" She could not miss the headline: Second Alaska Prince Engaged.

"Assumptions have been made," Rian said wryly. "I'm sorry. I'll have it redacted. You haven't said yes." Not to marrying him, not to *whatever.*

There was a photo of them, a photo from Florida. Tania was standing with the light streaming from behind her, as Rian, looking up at her…knelt at her feet. "You were only picking up my cane," she said in disbelief.

"Well, apparently, the Internet has jumped to many conclusions," Rian said, gesturing at his tablet.

"Is it bad?" Tania asked, exchanging her book for the newspaper and sinking into the chair beside the card catalog to read it.

"Depends on your definition of *bad*," Rian said. "Certain photos of me are back in circulation."

Tania let her hair fall over her face as she leaned over the paper, but not so fast that Rian didn't see the look of merriment and delight first. She had definitely seen *those* photos.

Then she looked up at him, grinning. "You have *nothing* to be embarrassed about," she told him, her voice rich with amusement.

"You didn't lose a bet," Rian muttered, but it was hard to sound angry when she looked so deliciously flustered.

"You're going to have to tell me the real story," Tania said firmly, eyes dancing. "There are about a hundred different versions of how it happened online. Did you lose a hockey game?"

"Do I look like I'd play hockey for nudity?" Rian scoffed. "Oh, no, it was much more personal."

"Well, you have to tell me *now!*" Tania wailed.

"Not a chance," Rian said, feigning stubbornness.

Tania gnashed her teeth at him playfully, then was sucked into the newspaper. "Oh my God," she said in horror. "How did they even find that out? They have my high school graduation photo?"

Rian watched her fascinating face as she read the article, wincing and shaking her head. "Well, they got some of it right," she said in exasperation. "Points for efforts. This also explains my mother's calls."

"Do you need to use a landline?" Rian offered at once.

"No, it's fine, I have an International plan," Tania said, shaking her head. "I just don't have the spoons to deal with my mother right now."

"What does that mean?" Rian asked. "You've said that before, about spoons. But last I checked, cutlery wasn't involved in phone calls."

She chuckled. "It's called the spoon theory. It started on the Internet, with someone trying to explain chronic illness to a friend. I start my day with a handful of spoons, and everything I do uses one up: taking a shower, making food, going to work, seeing a doctor, calling my mother... Healthy people have unlimited spoons, but I only get a few, so I have to decide how to use them and at the end of the day...I'm just *out* and unable to do anything."

"And I suppose forks aren't going to cut it."

"Don't think I haven't tried."

Rian absorbed the idea, trying to decide how much help she would want him to offer. "Your mom...you have a *fraught* relationship with her?"

Tania sighed. "My mother is not...good with boundaries. She is masterful at guilt trips and making everything about herself, about sucking people into her latest insult or imagined slight. She's kind of a hypochondriac, which is completely ironic because she thinks *I'm* faking *my* illness, and she doesn't make or keep friends easily, so she relies a lot on emotional support from her family. She thinks love is getting everyone to prove themselves by asking them to do things she can do herself, pretending to be helpless, that kind of thing. I learned a long time ago that anything I do is not enough, and that I have to be careful about overextending myself for her. I became much happier when I realized that it didn't really matter how quickly I answered her messages, I was never going to suddenly win her favor."

"She doesn't live in Florida?"

Tania shook her head. "She lives in New Jersey a few blocks from her sister, who is a lot more patient than I am. I sometimes feel guilty that Aunt Emilia puts up with so much from her, but if I learned boundaries, she can, too."

"Would you...want them to come here?" Rian asked reluctantly.

"Please don't ever even suggest the possibility," Tania said plaintively.

Rian bit back the logical next question about inviting them to the wedding. There *was* no wedding. Not yet.

She refolded the newspaper and put it back on the card catalog and curled back into the chair with her book. They exchanged a look, and Rian thought she was looking for permission to retreat. He granted it by picking up his own book and pulling the footrest into place.

He expected her presence to be distracting, but the treaty dissection he was reading was gritty and involved. It was based on the public version of the Compact, not the secret one, but the structure of the treaty was largely intact, and the author had some interesting observations about the trade relationships between the countries and some of the weirder restrictions.

They read in stillness for a while, and then Rian looked up to realize that Tania was flipping uninterestedly through her book, barely skimming it. "What are you reading?" he asked.

She closed it with a snap. "A dry introduction to legal language of the time that the Compact was written. Given what you've told me about magic and how it works, I thought it might be useful to see if there are some legal definitions for some of the words that have always given me pause. Things I always thought were just poetic might have meanings that I overlooked."

Rian wryly showed the cover to his own book. "I was hoping to find something, too," he admitted.

"I read that one," Tania said, not surprising him in the least. "The author likes to dwell on the historical conflicts from before the Compact. I guess Alaska and Majorca have always been at odds?"

"Not quite enemies," Rian said thoughtfully. "But...we've never had a particularly warm relationship. I've always thought that it was good that we were on opposite sides of the world."

"Do you get along with many of the other kingdoms? I mean, I know what the Internet says, but I figure there's a lot of friendly posturing."

Rian couldn't help thinking that Tania would make a more diplomatic queen than Carina. As little as he wanted to be king, she was smart and well-spoken, with careful words and measured responses.

"Alaska isn't that powerful politically," he said thoughtfully. "We don't curry favor with other countries or pursue alliances. But we have a lot of money and rich land. Generally the other Small Kingdoms are...polite to us."

"Suck-ups?" Tania suggested bluntly, and Rian had to laugh and reconsider his diplomatic assessment.

"Some, definitely. They would not be sorry to see our kingdom fall, or to carve up our resources according to the Compact. We've always had a really good relationship with Mo'orea; our parents were good friends. Genuinely friends, I mean, not just a show."

Tania was tapping the corner of the book against her mouth thoughtfully. "The Compact itself doesn't just forbid using magic against each other, it actually prevents it, right?"

Rian nodded. "Spells backfire. Disastrously."

"But there was a portal that got to the doors of your vault? Isn't *that* magic being used against you?"

"We could have enemies that aren't in the Compact," Rian suggested. "I mean, after Carina's big exposé last month, there's at least one giant corporation with a lot of powerful people gunning for us."

Tania put her book back in her lap. "Okay, there's another question I never thought to ask! How much magic is out there? Do countries other than the Small Kingdoms use it? Good grief, is the Constitution of the United States a spell?"

Rian shook his head. "I don't know that other Kingdoms *can't* use magic, but they don't. Or they keep it really quiet. Most treaties and historical documents are just that."

"And if Alaska fails to attend the Renewal?"

"Some of it is straight-forward; a country that didn't participate would be dropped from the protections. A lot of the Small Kingdoms' strength is in our alliance. None of us have large standing armies, but we are bound absolutely to support and defend each other. We can't enter war without a quorum, but if we do, we are too widespread, and too powerful together to discount. Not to mention the financial clout. If a country pissed off enough of the Small Kingdoms, they'd never get Cuban cigars or Japanese technology again. If we didn't have that alliance, the balance of power in the world would be very different."

"Canada isn't all that expansionistic," Tania said humorously.

"No, but there are many countries who are. Russia, just across the Bering Strait, would find us a juicy target. Did you study much of the Fifth Clause?"

"That was the part that defined all the internal trade considerations. Pretty dry stuff. I read it, but it was a slog, and I don't remember the details."

"Not just trade," Rian said. "There's some stuff that implies that, if circumstances are just right, the Small Kingdoms could redistribute the land of a nation caught in *contempt* of the Compact."

"I remember that part," Tania said, eyes narrow. "But they didn't define contempt." She eyed her book. "I suppose that failing to show up for the Renewal could be considered an example of contempt. So, there is plenty of motivation for someone within the Small Kingdoms to make sure that you didn't. But the magic in play indicates that it can't be someone from the Small Kingdoms, because the Compact can prevent that."

"Or they may have found a way to circumvent it."

"A loophole?"

"Or..." Rian considered. "Could the Compact itself be altered?"

"You have pages of the Compact in your vault," Tania reminded him. "The originals are divided among the Kingdoms and everyone has a paper copy of the full secret version." She frowned. "Is the copy magic, too?"

"Raval can explain better than I can," Rian said. "But the magic comes from the original and is...uh...augmented? by the copy. Enforced, maybe? Anchored?"

"You have to be careful of the word you choose," Tania teased him, waving her book. "Layers of meaning! Unintended implication!"

"I wouldn't put anything in writing," Rian chuckled. "Not without a lawyer and seven casters looking over it."

Tania was sitting at the edge of her seat, playing with the head of her cane. "*Can* the Compact be altered? I mean, it's just writing, right? Could you go in and change it? Could someone *else* have done that?"

Rian shuddered. "So much power, so many details, so many protections...it would take an amazing caster, way better than Raval or the Caster of the Guard, or anyone we know. I imagine erasing words would be inviting disaster."

"But changing just a word, here or there, it could be

done?" Tania pressed. "Like adding an ess to the word mate?"

Rian blinked at her. "Pluralize mate?"

"It could explain me," Tania said logically. "What if someone was trying to alter their page, for some kind of advantage. What if they made changes to their pages? You said it's *magic*, would it show up on the paper copies automatically? Like an operating system update?"

Rian struggled with the idea. "Raval says magic takes intention, it's not as simple as just writing down a single letter. Focus, power, the correct tool...he makes it sound like a whole huge ritual, won't let anyone watch when he does it. And I don't know if the copies would update or not. I'm not sure I want to test it."

"Can I see it? Maybe try to find changes? I mean, that's why I'm here." Rian stuffed down his fleeting wish that *he* was why she was here. Tania's face was lit up with excitement and Rian wondered if he was only sympathetically excited himself, if these were *her* feelings. Their bond seemed less intense than it had been, slowly fading away even as they became closer friends.

His dragon was unhelpful.

I thought you were supposed to be more in tune with magic, Rian grumbled at him. *Don't you know if this is me, or you, or her?*

She is our mate, his dragon insisted, as if that were the only thing that mattered.

"Do you really think you could find changes? If it's been updated, how would you know what was new?"

"If I had my old microfiche copies, I'd be able to compare them," Tania pointed out acidly, and Rian winced. "I know it's not your fault," she said apologetically. "That came out sharper than I meant."

"I know," Rian said, surprised that he did, and they were quiet for a moment.

"But...maybe I could remember?" Tania suggested. "Maybe looking at the pages would jog my memory or something? I...spent a lot of time poring over them."

"It's worth a try," Rian agreed. "I'll take you to the vault."

16

The guards who had fallen into step behind Tania and Rian stopped them at the top of the stairs going down from the first story. "Is she authorized to go down there?" one of them asked hesitantly. "We can't follow."

"She's my mate," Rian pointed out, and the guards exchanged dubious glances. "I vouch for her, and she'll be safe with me."

The guards spoke quietly a moment, radioed for permission while Tania tried not to fidget, and then finally nodded reluctantly. They took positions at the top of the stairs.

"They...can't come down here?" Tania said, holding Rian's hand and using her cane to tap down the wide, steep staircase with the other. They were walking down the center of the stairs, too far from the handrails, but Rian was steady beside her.

"There are a lot of things in the vault with power," Rian explained. "Including a dagger spelled to kill dragons, and the Compact itself. Ever since Shadow got in with

Carina, Fask and Captain Luke have been really strict; no one but family on the sub-level."

"I'm not family…" Tania pointed out, and Rian's hand in hers squeezed tighter.

"You're my mate," he said confidently, like he'd told the guards.

Mate. Tania almost stumbled, and focused fixedly on her feet for the next several steps. It was still surreal and impossible sometimes, when she thought too hard about things.

She'd been a nobody just a week ago. Worse than a nobody: a disabled, jobless, single woman with no prospects and a crumbled academic career.

Now, she was walking down restricted stairs to a dragon king's treasure vaults, her fingers twined together with a dragon prince. A dragon prince who looked at her like *she* was treasure. A dragon prince who was so beautiful that he took her breath away, and was somehow dearer even than his looks.

The stairs opened onto a wide hallway that appeared to be carved from granite streaked with veins of gold. It was lit intermittently with cool electric lights that made it look like it was a string of pearls—light and then dark and then light and then dark.

They walked for some time, at an easy pace, and then, although the hallway continued, they turned at a doorway with no latch or handle. It was perhaps ten feet tall, wooden, and carved all over with tiny letters. Tania let go of Rian's hand and started to reach for it, wondering how deep the letters were and what the wood would feel like, but Rian hissed a warning. "I don't know if that's a good idea."

Tania put her hand back at her side. Being his mate

might be good enough for the guards, but not for this spell, perhaps.

Rian put his own hand flat on the door and said his full name, "Prianriakist."

Tania memorized the syllables with relish; she'd never heard his full name pronounced, and it made something resonate in her chest.

The door cracked open soundlessly, and Rian pushed it open. Tania was captured for a moment by the thickness of it, and the fact that as it opened and the light fell across it, it was clear that the fine carving was unexpectedly deep, the bottom of each letter lost in darkness.

Then she saw the hoard beyond and she gaped in astonishment, clinging to her cane with both hands.

It was the kind of hoard that fantasy books and fairy tales only imagined. The cave was the size of a warehouse, stretching organically in every direction past the door, and it was filled with treasure.

"Smaug's treasure had nothing on this," she observed, when she could make her feet carry her in.

Rian looked pleased, and a little shy.

In the center were heaps of shining coins and drapes of jewels, cups and rings and gleaming nets of silver hung with bells. There were tables, in places, showcasing particularly fine items: antique vases and pieces of fragile art.

Amazed and a little intimidated, Tania followed Rian through a maze of piles and displays, boggling over the combined value and rarity of the things she was seeing. She didn't offer to touch any of it.

A table that appeared to be carved from jade held a huge glass dome, and within that, Tania recognized the Compact. There were two piles; a paper copy, and fewer, thicker pages than Tania knew must be the originals.

"Sheepskin parchment?" she guessed, bending in awe to look at them through the crystal-clear glass.

"Dragonskin," Rian said, grimly.

Tania's breath caught in her throat. The hoard had satisfied some of her desire to witness magic, but she still hadn't seen any of them as dragons, and she was dying to, even while it felt very awkward and invasive to ask.

"*Whose* dragonskin? What are its properties? Do the oils of human hands damage it? Do you have gloves? Can I touch it?"

Rian chuckled, and lifted the glass effortlessly, even though Tania guessed that it must be very heavy. "It is said that the first dragon sacrificed its immortality for the document, draining the magic of the world at the time to create it."

He put the glass cover to one side and lifted the stack of papers. "Do you want the originals, too? You can't hurt them."

"Yes," Tania said promptly. "Can I?!"

She stretched out her arms, but realized swiftly that she couldn't carry the pages and her cane at the same time.

"Hang on..." Rian glanced around, leaving the Compact on the edge of the table, and then vanished into the aisles of treasure.

Tania stepped up to the table and hesitantly touched the top page of the copy, ready to snatch her hand back at the slightest snap of power or resistance.

Magic, she thought in awe, and she was filled with a bittersweet rush of amazement and wonder. So much of her life she'd spent puzzling over the language of this document, trying to unlock its mysteries with only half a key, and now she was standing next to a copy so old that she could smell its age, and some of the original pages.

On *dragonskin*.

Made from *magic*.

What *was* this world, even?

"Here," Rian said, reappearing. He was holding a leather satchel, just thick enough to hold all of the pages. It seemed to be edged in gold filigree, and the leather was etched all over in beautiful patterns.

"Is it okay if I use that?" Tania asked, staring. "I mean…ah…I don't know how a royal hoard works. Do I pay a deposit?" She'd priced luggage a few years previous and been astonished at the prices of just some canvas and steel pieces. And this was almost more of a work of art than a piece of baggage.

"This is from my personal hoard," Rian assured her, shrugging one shoulder towards one of the far corners. He carefully unbuckled the bag and tucked the contract into it.

Tania could not resist asking, "What else is in your hoard?"

Rian flushed and looked like she'd just asked to see his porno stash. Maybe she had. "You don't have to say."

"No," he said quickly. "I'd like to show you…"

They picked through mountains of chains of precious metal and past a series of statues that must be from ancient Greece to the far end of the cave. "Has your family…been collecting this for long?" Tania asked, eyeing what looked like one of the Easter island heads. She wasn't sure how to diplomatically ask if the pieces had been stolen or looted, but Rian guessed her direction at once.

"Everything here is paid for," he said swiftly. "No dragon wants treasure laden with debt." Then he added, "Well, no Alaskan dragon. Not all of the Small Kingdoms are quite as honorable."

"Where did your wealth come from?" Tania couldn't resist asking. "Originally."

"There are stories," Rian said, as he led her to a cave

off from the others, neatly filled with free-standing bookshelves filled with old books. "Some people say that the dragons won a bet, or maybe did a favor, and were rewarded in fae gold. The stories are so old and muddled, it's hard to know what's true, but my ancestors invested wisely."

"But fairy gold...doesn't last?" Tania dragged a finger down the nearest row of books and picked one at random. "You have this upstairs."

"A reprint. This is the original."

"First edition?" Tania said, opening to the title page. A signature was scrawled illegibly under the title.

"First edition, signed, *and* the first copy off the press," Rian said smugly. "There's a certificate in the back."

Tania whistled and wished she were wearing gloves, replacing the book carefully.

It wasn't just randomly rare books, she recognized, scanning the titles, it was a curated collection that reflected Rian's taste: classics, science fiction, non-fiction on specific topics, and... "You must have every book about dragons that was ever written." She caressed a set of custom leather spines on McCaffrey's Dragonriders series.

Rian flushed. "It's a hobby," he said sheepishly. "I like to see what they get right."

"Do they get much right?"

Rian grinned. "Not really."

Tania had wandered to the end of one of the aisles and turned to walk down the next one. These shelves were covered in antique bottles and glasses. Beer, wine, classic sodas, bottles so old and sea-worn that they were impossible to identify.

"Aren't you worried about earthquakes?" she asked, not offering to touch any of them. Before Rian could answer, she guessed, "I suppose there's a spell on them."

He nodded. "The whole hoard has a motion-protection spell. It's keyed to the room, so everything is covered. The entire castle above could fall down and this cave would barely rattle."

"Raval's work?" Tania asked curiously.

"Before Raval's time, like the door," Rian said. "And honestly beyond his skills. Possibly beyond the magic of the world today."

"I'd like to talk with him about the Compact some time," Tania said. "Ask him some of the magic questions you haven't been able to answer."

"Sure," Rian promised. "Raval's a little gruff, but you get used to him, and he'll help out if he can."

17

When Rian had warned her that Raval was a "little gruff," Tania was expecting that he'd be shy or perhaps impatient with her stupid newbie questions about magic.

She was not expecting him to throw an engine part at her the following day.

Fortunately, Rian had reflexes like a cat...or a dragon, Tania supposed...and he caught the flying chunk of metal while Tania was still trying to decide if she should drop her cane to try to cover her face and risk falling.

The whole thing was over in a split second, and Tania was taking stock of the fact that she had not been hit. Her whole body was in panic-mode, and she knew that her simple act of freezing was going to mean a rough night.

"What the hell, Raval?" Rian demanded, hurling the part back. They were in the back room of the garage, where Raval was perched like a mad scientist at a workbench with a screaming Dremel in his hands.

Raval caught the thing with the same lightning reflexes that Rian had demonstrated. He looked distinctly wild around the eyes, and he stared at them for several moments without apparently actually seeing them. Then he shook his head, exhaling like he'd been holding his breath.

He powered down the Dremel. "Sorry," he said, and that was more the gruff that Tania had expected. "I didn't hear you coming."

"You could have *hurt* her," Rian snarled.

Raval's face shuttered. "Shouldn't interrupt," he growled back. "Never interrupt."

Tania was thinking that they *really* shouldn't. "We could come back later." *Never,* she privately thought.

"Tania has questions about magic."

Raval shrugged one shoulder and sighed.

Was that her cue to speak? Her mind seemed blank and Raval was completely uninviting. It was hard to remember that he was Rian's brother; Rian was so warm and funny. Raval was cold and expressionless.

"I was...ah...just wondering a few things about magic. The Compact, mostly," she stammered. "Rian told me a little about how magic works, with...ah...intentions and focus and words. How spells fade once they're used, and of course, I'm familiar with the Compact."

Raval grunted and Tania realized she hadn't asked any questions.

"I...ah...wanted to know if you could alter a spell, once it was cast. We were talking about the break-in, and whether other members of the Small Kingdoms could alter their pages and what that would do. And if that would change the paper copies?"

Then Raval really did have expressions: utter horror and disbelief. "You could absolutely *not* do that. That would be...like a librarian trying to do brain surgery on a person without anesthesia."

"You know, they do brain surgeries without anesthesia for some disorders," Rian pointed out.

"It's an analogy, idiot," Raval said, scowling. He glared at Tania again. "Only the caster knows the *intention*. That's why no spell is the same, even if you copy it word-for-word. If you start mucking around in someone else's spells, you can't know what chaos you'll unleash. The one letter you're adding may tip a whole sentence into new meaning and unlock an underlying desire or unknown trigger. It's not just *language*."

He said it like Tania ought to already know that, but that prompted another idea that she had been stewing over. "Language! That was another question I had! Why is the Compact in English? That was always one of my biggest confusions. Why isn't it in an older language? At the time it was written, English wasn't that widespread; Spanish and Portuguese were more common, and if you wanted something classical, why not Latin? Some of the phrases are a little dated or stilted, but it's very clearly not even in medieval English; it's all bafflingly modern. I thought it was just that I was looking at a translation, but the original pages are exactly the same."

Raval laughed, but Tania felt like it wasn't unkind. "The Compact is layers and layers of spells. One of them simply puts itself into a common language. Someone whose first language is Greek would be wondering why the first dragons put the Compact in *their* own language. Which would also complicate your idea that someone could alter it. An alteration in what they see might not translate well."

The idea was staggering. "Everyone sees a different Compact?"

"It's the same Compact," Raval corrected. "It's just that the Compact chooses what you see."

"Like...selecting the language interface setting in a computer program?"

Raval considered. "Sort of. More like viewing a computer program through a compiler, where what you are seeing isn't the raw code, but an output of data calls and discrete programs."

Tania only understood about half of that. She was beginning to sway in place; between her focus, and her fright upon their entrance, she could feel her hip beginning to ache.

Rian noticed almost as soon as she did. "Do you need a chair?"

Tania gratefully accepted a swivel shop chair. It wasn't the kind she could sit in comfortably for any length of time, but it beat trying to stay on her own feet. "So, do two people who view the Compact and speak the same language see the exact same words if they have different technical backgrounds? Like...a lawyer has specific meanings for some words that a scientist might not agree with."

"It's according to who reads it," Raval said, pulling up his own chair with enviable grace. "I haven't actually tested it, but I would guess that the lawyer would get one version and a linguist would see a slightly different one."

"Then how can there be arbitration *of* the Compact? You don't have the same words to compare!"

"The Compact is its own arbitrator," Raval pointed out. "It is enforced by...well...by itself. With magic. It is always read exactly as it was intended, and it metes out its own punishments."

"Ah..." Tania said. "That makes some sense." She gazed over Raval's workbench. Most of what lay there was unrecognizable; bits and pieces of an engine, perhaps, etched all over with tiny letters. It was a curious combination of chaos and absolute order. "When you do magic, do you do that, too? The language thing, I mean."

Raval snorted. "That is something so beyond casters of our day that it would be impossible."

"Have you got that piece of the spell that they found at the scene of the break-in?" Rian wanted to know.

Raval pushed his chair, on wheels, back to a toolbox behind him and removed a small, flat box from one of the drawers. The thick paper he drew from it was just a strip and it was entirely blackened; one edge had clearly burned away. Spidery letters were barely visible through the soot. He put it down with focused care in front of Rian and Tania, carefully making it perfectly straight on the table.

It was in Spanish and Tania found herself marveling again over the idea of a spell so complex that it could translate itself. This must be an order of magnitude simpler than the Compact, and the caster must have simply written it in their native language.

"This part of the spell wasn't used," Raval pointed out, like he wasn't sure if Tania would pick up on the fact. "That's where mates are referenced."

"Mates?" Tania asked sharply. "Plural?"

"Mates," Raval said shortly. "Plural."

Tania's Spanish wasn't great; her grandmother had solely spoken the language when she was a child, but at her death, her mother had stopped using it altogether. She had some basic conversational Spanish, but nothing technical. Between that, the handwriting, and the smoke smudging, it was hard to make out any words. "I expected it to be more...legible," Tania complained. "If it's done with so much intention, why isn't it *neater*?" That had been one of the things that had delighted her about the Compact; it was absolutely gorgeously written, with tiny, tidy writing given just the slightest hint of swirl.

Raval scowled at her. "Intention of magic, not intention of satisfying a teacher. No one actually *has* to be able to read it, it's just that language gives most people a structure to hang their intentions on."

Tania bit her lip and handed back the scorched paper. "Can I...can I see some magic?" It was a hard question to ask, but Raval seemed to be expecting it, and he gave her a wry smile.

"Dance, monkey," he muttered to himself, shaking his head. Then he reached into a drawer and pulled out a gray stone carved all over with tiny, perfect lettering. He dropped it into Tania's hand and then said, carefully, "Warmth."

The stone heated, so abruptly that Tania almost dropped it. But it didn't get uncomfortably hot, just soothingly warm. "Thank you!" she said.

"Stop," Raval said, and it seemed to revert back to a simple rock. "That's a fairly basic spell," he said, holding out his hand for it. "Only took a month or two to make, probably good for another dozen uses." He rubbed a thumb over the letters.

Feeling guilty for wasting one of them, Tania handed the stone back and gave a hiss of discomfort as the chair rotated unexpectedly beneath her. Rian didn't miss the noise. "Thanks, Raval," he said, rising to his feet. "You've been helpful."

"Any time," Raval said wryly. "But you should text first or something."

"There was one more thing," Tania remembered. "Supposing the originals were altered, would the copies update? Like an operating system update on your phone or laptop?"

Raval shrugged. "The repercussions are too dear," he assured her. "No one would be willing to test it and risk that kind of backlash." He bent back to his work dismissively.

As Tania pulled her hood up over her head to walk back to the castle, she leaned on Rian. He was so solid and comfortable at her side. She was starting to feel like he had always been there, that he would always be there, such a feeling of sanctuary to just having him near.

"I keep thinking about changing the Compact," she said thoughtfully. It was snowing, and they paused for a moment on the back deck, looking out at the wide yard and the picturesque forest beyond.

"Raval seems to think alteration would be unlikely."

"What would *destroying* the pages do?"

The idea seemed to draw Rian up. "I imagine, if we're going to follow our computer program analogy, that it would be like deleting a chunk of code. The remaining system may still work but would be buggy, or it could fail altogether."

"Leaving the world in chaos and Alaska undefended. Big job for one little treaty," Tania observed. She shivered, and Rian put his arm around her.

"Come inside and warm up," he suggested.

They walked the rest of the way to the castle nestled close together, and Tania's head was full of magic and history.

18

The next several days were a blur. Tania had her hair done, and her nails, and got a massage, all at Carina's insistence.

"How would you like your hair?" the beautician asked her, not offering the slightest hint of judgement for Tania's unkempt locks. "Shall we continue the blond highlights, or cover them and go natural? Perhaps a different color altogether?"

Tania looked at Carina, flipping through one of the style sample folders. She was naturally, effortlessly blonde, and Tania felt a moment of stubbornness. "Let's go dark," she said boldly. She didn't need to try to be something she wasn't.

"I love it," Carina said in warm approval. "You've got such gorgeous natural coloring. Just a little more blond at the top for me," she said, glancing at herself in the mirror. "Nothing major, just match the colors in the rest of this mop and pretend I haven't been cooped up in a sunless castle for a month. And a haircut, definitely."

Tania left the room that was set up as their spa feeling

like she'd been through an elaborate version of slow torture, but her hair whispered in healthy waves over her shoulders again, and Rian's face when she saw him in the hallway before lunch was worth the effort.

"I decided to ditch the blond," she said, almost sheepishly, though his eyes were lit up with delight.

"It's perfect," he said gruffly, locking his hands behind him like he was afraid he'd reach out and touch her without meaning to. "Beautiful. Different. Amazing."

"My twin, the thesaurus," Tray said mockingly, elbowing past to get to his seat.

Lunch was grueling, but Tania was buoyed by Rian's helpless glances and flushes, and the flutter of her own hair against her neck. She smelled different. Better. Fancier.

More *queenly*.

Toren, across the table with Carina, made no bones about loving her make-over. "You smell like gardens," he declared, putting his entire face into her hair and sniffing deeply. "It's like summer on your head."

After the meal, which was mostly jokes and casual conversation centered around the food, Carina invited Tania to visit the puppies again. Tania would have preferred a nap, but cuddling with the tiny, still-unnamed puppy was some of the best therapy that she had ever enjoyed. Probably-Moose romped with her brothers and made Carina laugh until tears were spilling from her eyes, but Tania's little fawn-colored sister was content to play with the string from Tania's hoody and gnaw on her finger.

The humans, four puppies, and a tired mama dog spent refreshing moments laughing and talking about nothing. Then, as the puppies began to wind down and the short Alaskan winter day turned into that curious endless twilight of evening, Carina helped Tania to her feet. "We've got a press conference tomorrow at the opening ceremony for a clinic in Fairbanks," she said cheerfully. "People want to meet you."

"We do? They do?" Tania had been hoping that the following day would be a day to recover from this day. Carina clearly thought that it had been a day of rest, but Tania could feel the exhaustion like a looming reaper, following her around everywhere with icy fingers of doom, something she always had trouble admitting. "Do I *have* to?" It sounded ungrateful, after everything that had been done for her. She refrained from pointing out that she hadn't even agreed to marry Rian yet.

"It won't be so bad," Carina promised. "Fask will give you notes if you want to just read them from the cards. It's a good cause, we're donating some money, and it will be low-key because Captain Luke isn't letting riff-raff in."

"Except the riff-raff that's already in," Tania said with a chuckle.

"Well, *that* riff-raff is royalty," Carina said archly. "She has to let *them* in."

Tania exchanged a grin with Carina as they walked back to the main hallways of the castle. It was clear that she was slow, compared to Carina, but the crown-princess-to-be kept her pace thoughtfully restrained.

"Second floor or third?" Carina asked pointedly at the landing of the second floor.

"*My* room," Tania said wryly. They walked down the hall.

The room Carina shared with Toren was just down the hallway from her own door, but Carina paused with her and hesitantly asked, "Did you ever believe in destiny? Before all of this, I mean?"

"I'm not sure I do now," Tania said frankly. "I believe in free will, you know? I always thought that fiction that relied too heavily on fate and prophecy was taking the easy path, sort of cheating."

"You don't think that the Compact knows the future?"

Tania wished she wasn't running out of energy so fast; she would have liked to take the time to invite Carina in and have this conversation in earnest. The more she got to know Carina, the more she liked her, and right now, she looked vulnerable and uncertain and Tania kind of wanted to hug her.

"I...don't know," she confessed. "When I met Rian, he told me that all those things I was feeling were what I was *going* to feel, like an echo from the future. And that's a kind of a terrifying idea, that a piece of paper can make me feel things in the first place, before you even add in the concept of an immutable future."

"I can't untangle them anymore," Carina admitted. "Did I fall in love with Toren because I was convinced I would? Or was I convinced that I would because I already had? Or..." she laughed helplessly. "I can't even wrap my head around it sometimes."

"Are you sorry?" It was a terrifically personal thing to ask, but the words were out of Tania's mouth before she could stop them; being tired sometimes made her blurt things out. It was certainly not a great trait for a queen!

"No," Carina said at once, earnestly. "Not even a little. I mean, there were some rather horrible moments, what with people trying to kill us, but...it's not even being a princess; I could care less about that, I'd be a pauper to be with Toren. He's so everything I never even knew I *wanted*. I feel like I kind of have to believe in destiny, because he's absolutely perfect for me and I feel so safe and happy with him."

Tania felt longing rise up in her chest and threaten to steal away her breath. She felt exactly that way about

Rian, that he was exactly what she'd always wanted and never even thought to dream of, that she felt safe and happy with him, that she craved him impossibly when she wasn't with him. "It's a lot to take in," she said softly. "But, *yeah*…"

"You two are great together," Carina said, smiling. "And it's adorable watching you pretend not to pine after each other."

Tania flushed, dismayed to think that she'd been so transparent. "It's not...we're not...I mean…"

"Why not?" Carina needled. "He's a gorgeous Alaskan prince who adores you! What are you waiting around for?"

"I think I hear my phone ringing," Tania said desperately. "Thank you for the spa day, I love your hair, probably going to take a long nap after that massage, gotta go…"

Carina, not the slightest bit fooled, laughed merrily and moved on down the hallway. "We'll talk more later!" Two of the guards that had been lingering at the end of the hall respectfully out of earshot peeled off to follow her to her door. "See you tomorrow morning! They'll want to do some makeup and publicity shots before the reception!"

Tania felt dread overcome her fluster as she closed her door behind her.

Fask had indeed supplied notecards; they were neatly-written and waiting for her in the sitting room, with a newly-tailored skirt-suit and a pair of low-heeled shoes. Tania, suddenly overcome with exhaustion, didn't touch any of them, only staggered for her bed to try to regain enough energy for dinner.

19

"She's a natural," Fask said approvingly to Rian.

Carina and Tania were holding court with the small audience and press members following their presentation to the new health center of the oversized check.

Rian wasn't sure that Tania had wanted to be involved in the event; the magical pull of the mate-bond had eased, so he had to figure out her expressions and body language. Carina was convincing, and Tania had shyly accepted before Rian could figure out how boorish it would be to intervene and make Carina stop pestering her.

Tania hadn't made a single word of complaint, and had practiced her speech several times with Rian. She hadn't seemed overly nervous about it.

And the audience *loved* them.

After the short presentation, there had been a reception of top local officials, press, and health center staff, reluctantly approved by Captain Luke, and the two women had been the center of all the attention, holding careful court near the refreshment table as they made small talk.

Fask, Rian, and Toren let the women dominate the stage, hanging back to let them shine, and Fask was right, Tania *was* a natural. She was unfailingly polite and just slightly shy as she conversed with important figures, and she looked even more royal and confident than Carina did.

"I knew she'd be good at this," Rian said to Fask, trying not to worry for her unnecessarily. Did she sway a little? She had decided against carrying a cane, hoping that the short duration would mean she wouldn't need it, and Rian knew how much she detested the symbol of her weakness and how ugly she thought her cane was. "She's smart, and educated, and she's got such a big heart. I don't think there's anything she *can't* do."

"Are you going to make it official soon?" That was from one of the council members, a pompous white-bearded man who played Santa Claus every year at the holiday parties that Rian dreaded. "I'd understand if you didn't want to tread on your brother's good news, of course."

Rian gave the man a long look. The council didn't know about *mates* as more than an archaic name for the intended of the heir, of course, but the rumor that Rian and Tania were an *item of interest* was persistent and no one had actually attempted to contradict it. It was hard to deny that something was afoot when the Internet was filled with photos of them holding hands and smiling besottedly at each other. "Nothing official," he said mildly.

"I suppose it's kind of you to allow the younger brother his time as crown prince," the official said with a knowing laugh. "Before you get saddled with all the responsibility."

That caused a frown to fold Rian's eyebrows. "That's not necessarily..." He stopped himself. The topic was too complicated for this company, so he smiled blandly. "We'll cross that bridge when we get to it," he said with just a hint of steel.

He was still watching Tania, though he was trying not to be obvious about it, and this time he thought she really was swaying a little in place.

We should go to her, his dragon insisted.

She was laughing with some of the nurses, and she didn't look distressed, so Rian thought his concern must be misplaced. But he couldn't keep the worry from spreading through his chest as she continued to converse merrily.

She's got this, he assured his dragon against his better judgement.

At that moment, Fask asked him a question to draw him back into the conversation and Rian had to pay attention to the small talk again.

It would be too forward to go save her, anyway; he would look too possessive. He thought over what she'd done already that afternoon. He'd gotten a good idea of how much she could do in a day, observing how she flagged if there were certain strains or too many tasks to handle; he had actually been able to *feel* when she was struggling at first, even while she was putting on a brave face and trying to pretend she could handle it all.

He wasn't confident that she *couldn't* handle this, and he didn't want to undermine her autonomy. Was the glance she gave in his direction a plea for help?

His dragon gave a wordless fuss, and Rian tried to convince himself that his dragon wasn't any more sensitive to their mate's state than he was, just more of a worrywart.

The Santa Claus official had made some kind of joke and Rian missed his cue to laugh, though Fask and Toren both did. He came in too late and sounded awkward, but he didn't care, because he was watching Tania again. He was sure from her body language that she was in increasing pain, but he still wasn't sure enough to go barge into her moment of celebrity. It was driving him crazy.

"Excuse me," he finally said, though it had probably been obvious for some time that he wasn't tracking the conversation at all.

The crowd seemed to deliberately swirl between him and the refreshment table, and he had to stop to make conversational noises at several people before he was able to wind between them and finally see a clear path to Tania.

And he knew as soon as he lay eyes on her again that he was too late.

Her smile was as sweet as ever, but she was pale under her naturally bronze skin and the area around her eyes was just a little too tight. Then someone spoke behind her and she jerked like she'd been jolted with electricity and grabbed for the edge of the table, too far away.

Rian could not close the space between them fast enough to catch her as he watched her try to twist and keep herself upright, unsuccessfully, only hurting herself worse, he was sure.

There was a crash of platters as she fell and pulled part of the buffet with her, and Rian had to manhandle someone out of the way when they stepped between him and his mate, exclaiming in surprise.

"Are you okay?" he asked uselessly, elbowing past Carina, who was asking the same useless thing.

Tania was pale and flushed all at once, but she was trying too brightly to laugh. "I'm sorry," she said. "I'm just...clumsy."

Rian knelt next to her.

"Should have brought my ugly cane," she said regretfully, in a voice so small even he could barely hear her.

"I should have come and gotten you sooner," Rian growled, angry with himself.

"I thought I could…"

Rian had an arm under hers and pulled her effortlessly

to her feet, as slowly and carefully as he could manage. "I should have known."

"I'm sorry," she said quietly.

Rian scowled at anyone who got in their way, and glanced over to see Tania wearing a desperate smile that did nothing to mask her mortification. Several people snapped photos on their phone as he all but carried her slowly from the room.

The guards called the car and met them at the door with her coat, and Rian carefully laid it over her shoulders and helped her into the back seat, crawled in beside her, and drew her into his arms, where she went limp.

"I'm sorry," she repeated. "I thought I could do this. It's ridiculous that I can't." Her voice was full of frustration and tears.

"It's not your fault," Rian assured her, stroking her arms. "I asked too much."

"It shouldn't be too much!" Tania cried. "I should be able to have my hair done and spend a few hours walking around a room eating finger food! I should be able to go a full day without needing a nap like a toddler! I should be able to do *two* things in an afternoon, not just hope that I don't need to make a phone call and lose my entire day! Why can't I do these things? Why can't I be well?"

Rian didn't even try to answer her questions, just held her as gently as he could while they drove back to the castle and parked in front without getting out. He waved away the guard who tried to open their door.

"You don't have to do any of those things," he assured her. "You don't have to prove anything. You don't have to *do* anything."

She wept into his shoulder until she went limp, and Rian could feel her exhaustion and misery as if they were still freshly bound.

"What am I going to do?" she asked wearily.

"You're going to go to bed," Rian said firmly. "You're going to take whatever you need and sleep as long as you want, and tomorrow, I'm going to run away with you to the hot springs, where you will do nothing but nap and soak in mineral pools and if I have to carry you around in my arms, well, Toren shouldn't have all the fun." Photos of his brother carrying Carina out of the hot pools had been spread around on the Internet on the first day they met.

"What about the Compact?" Tania asked plaintively. "I should be studying it. Talking more to Raval about how magic works. Figuring out the succession questions. It's why I'm *here*."

"We'll take it with us," Rian said, trying not to wish again that *he* was the reason she was there. "The resort has already cleared out for the wedding and security is in place; it wouldn't be any safer if we left it here. And you don't have to so much as glance at it unless you feel like it."

Behind them, another car pulled up and Rian looked back to find that Toren and Carina had caught up with them.

Tania sat up and wiped her eyes. Her careful eye makeup had smudged around her eyes, emphasizing how hollow they looked. "I must be a mess," she said sadly. "I'm so...sorry."

Rian took her face in both of his hands. "You are not a mess. You are a miracle. You are the bravest person I know and I don't know how you get up every morning. I am in awe of your strength, of your persistence against terrible odds." He rubbed away one of the tears on her cheeks and kissed her gently on the forehead. "Want me to carry you in?"

"Goodness no," Tania said, her face cracking into a smile at last. "Let me have some dignity."

"Oh, Tania," Carina greeted them, when Rian helped Tania out of the car. "Are you alright? I'm so sorry, I should have gotten us out of that painful conversation sooner. I was just oblivious, are you *okay*?"

"Yes, of course," Tania said, but she made no bones about clinging to Rian's arm on the freshly shoveled sidewalk leading up to the castle.

"Oh," Toren said merrily, when they got to the bottom of the stairs, "here's your chance to carry her in."

"No, I..." Tania protested.

"It's easy, I'll show you!" Toren swept Carina into his arms as she flailed in surprise and pounded on his shoulders.

"Put me down, you oaf!" she yelled. "What are you doing?!" She was laughing and clinging to him as much as she was protesting, clearly enjoying herself.

Rian let Toren carry Carina up the front steps, going slowly with a chuckling Tania. "I could do that if you wanted," he suggested too quietly for anyone else to hear.

"I'm not that desperate," she said crisply.

But when they got into the house, shaking snow from their shoes, she looked at the next flight of stairs with loathing. Toren and Carina didn't wait for them, disappearing up into the castle with teasing shouts. "How far away did you say the elevator was?"

Rian took a chance as he was taking her coat and offered again, "If you want..."

"No, I've got this."

They took it slowly, step by step, and the guards went ahead and opened the door to her room, shutting it after they went in.

Rian took her straight to her bed, where she crawled with a little whimper and lay down looking like she'd just run a marathon.

"What can I get for you? What can I do?"

"Shoes," Tania whispered. "I should never have worn those shoes."

Rian wasn't much of a judge of shoes, but they didn't seem nearly as severe as most women's shoes, with low heels and rounded toes. He slipped them carefully off her feet, trying not to trail his fingers along her feet; she'd worn thin tights, in deference to the snowy weather, but they did nothing to hide the shapely lines of her legs.

"Now, what do I get you?" Rian wanted to know, chucking the shoes directly into the trash can just inside the bathroom.

She laughed at that, and directed him to the pills on the counter. Rian brought them all to her, sweeping them into his arms, and let her pick through and decide what to take while he poured her a glass of water.

"Do they work?" he asked dubiously, eying the labels as he took them back to the bathroom for her.

"For some definitions of *work*," Tania said miserably, sitting up to take them and then collapsing back into her pillow. "Eventually. But they don't leave me good for much else."

"Want me to pick back up with the time traveling highlander book?" Rian offered.

Tania shook her head. "I won't be able to follow it for long," she said with resignation. "You don't have to stay."

"May I?"

She looked at him in confusion. "May you what?"

"Stay," Rian said. "May I stay with you until you fall asleep? If it's not too creepy."

"No..." she said, looking at him curiously. "It's not creepy, because I want you here."

Rian dragged a chair in from the sitting room and made a show of kicking off his shoes, then he gathered

Tania's hand into his own and they sat quietly for a little while.

"Has it always been like this?" Rian finally asked, making little patterns on the back of her hand with his thumb.

"I was actually in track and field in high school," Tania said wryly. "I liked to go jogging with my girlfriends. It wasn't until I was a senior that things started going sideways. It was like I suddenly got clumsy. I took a spill water-skiing and didn't bounce back like I expected to. I got x-rays, nothing was broken, no one ever found anything wrong, but my right hip has never been the same. At first, after that, I thought it was just the pain wearing me down; it was never awful, it was just never-ending. But after a few months, I realized that the fatigue was more than just being a little tired and depressed. It wasn't all at once, or right away, it was only about a year ago it got really bad, and I was really good at fighting through it. I graduated, started my masters, worked at the library…"

"…Had your thesis torpedoed by mysterious masked ninjas…"

Tania giggled. "Did they really wear masks?"

"Probably not," Rian admitted. "But they might have been ninjas. Japan is one of the Small Kingdoms, and they may still have them. They might not technically call them ninjas anymore, though."

"See, that's a little comforting," Tania said. "If you're going to fail, it's at least not that shameful to fail because ninjas stole your work."

"You didn't fail," Rian said automatically. "Your work was brilliant."

Tania didn't try to argue the point.

"Can I get you a specialist?" Rian asked, hoping it was a courteous offer. "I mean, I could find you one. The best in the country. In the world. Being a prince has to be worth something."

Tania looked at him with tears gathering in her eyes. "I don't know what they could do," she said. "It's not like TV, where they figure out what's wrong with you and how to fix it in one neat episode. A lot of these things, they don't have a better diagnosis than 'well, we've eliminated most things, it's probably one of these other things, but none of them have effective treatments you can afford anyway. Take some aspirin and try to lose some weight.'"

"I kind of want to punch every one of those doctors," Rian admitted.

Tania giggled again. "Believe me, I get it."

She looked more comfortable now, heavy-eyed and smiling faintly. He gently rubbed the back of her hand until her eyelashes fluttered down over her cheeks and her breathing evened.

Rian sat with her a long moment longer, then tucked the comforter up around her and kissed her forehead. He turned off the lamp beside the bed and then sat in the dark room with her a little longer, unwilling to leave.

She was so dear, so tangled in his heart. Rian hadn't expected her to remain so deep under his skin as the magic of the Compact faded.

She is ours, his dragon said, in perfect contentment.

But she hadn't said *yes*.

20

"Are you *sure* about this?" Tania stared in horror at the frosted door. It had been so cold coming into the pool house that her nose-hairs felt like they had frozen, and she'd been wearing *clothing* at that time.

Now here she was, dressed in nothing more than a swimsuit, with bare feet on cool tile. The room they were in was warm and moist, but there was *ice* on the doors and windows. And Rian wanted her to go *outside*.

"These tubs look just fine," she said weakly, gesturing to the indoor pools.

"You'll love it," Rian assured her, his arm solid under her hand. He was terrifically distracting, in his boxer-style blue bathing suit and absolutely nothing hiding his gorgeous upper body and legs. He was even better in person than he'd been in the nude photos on the Internet: perfectly, effortlessly sculpted. "Are you ready?"

Ready to run out there into the freezing cold? Ready to slide over a path of ice risking life and limb? Tania was definitely not ready. "Yes," she squeaked anyway.

She left her cane behind, trusting Rian to get her safely

back in. She had a moment of picturing herself being carried inside folded up in an ice cube, cartoon-style. Then Rian was opening the door in a rush of fog and freezing air, leading her carefully forward.

The journey to the outdoor pool was every bit as awful as Tania had imagined, and she got to the water's edge shivering and wondering how she had come to this. Only the warmth of Rian at her side kept her from turning around and fleeing back the way she'd come. All of her muscles were tight. This was a *terrible* idea.

Then she dipped a toe cautiously into the warm water. "Oh," she said in awe, and then Rian was drawing her down the ramp into the pool, wading until they could float.

It was like being wrapped in hot silk, slowly sinking into the water, and Tania could feel the heat penetrating to her very bones.

Carina and Toren had already splashed into the pool, and were making out rather conspicuously at the far end. She couldn't see them, but their sounds through the fog were unmistakable.

"No pressure," Rian muttered, letting go of Tania self-consciously.

She caught his gaze and laughed at him as he led the way to a separate little rock-shaped cove, both of them half-swimming, half-wading easily through the water. It was hard to make out the shape of the pool through the dense steam rising from the hot water, but Tania thought it was generally like a three-leafed clover, with pockets where small groups of people could sit and soak. The pool was deserted, except for the four of them. Tania guessed, by the capacity signs, that this was not at all the usual state.

She was keenly aware of Rian, as they talked idly about books, and caught him ripping his gaze away from her several times. She had to be careful, not to let herself stare. Drifting in the dim, rosy twilight, shrouded in steam, everything seemed enchanted, and she kept thinking about how beautiful he was, and how much he adored her.

Out of it all, the magic, and the dragons, and the royalty, the thing she trusted the most was that Rian cared for her. She knew that magic faded, but what was between them felt solid and true, seated in trust and...love.

Then she'd steal a look at him, and he'd look away, and she'd wonder how this was even her life.

They floated near each other, and brushed each other once, and Tania thought they might even kiss, but the moment passed and Carina and Toren came splashing through the fog, giggling in a terribly un-royal way.

"Oh, your hair!" Carina laughed, when they came into view.

Tania reached up and realized that her hair was frosted solid around her face, stiff to the touch, and cold. Carina's blond hair had frost in it, too, but Tania imagined it was more striking in her own dark locks.

"Will it hurt my hair?" she asked in alarm, only thinking afterward that it might sound vain.

"Nah," Toren said easily. He had a little frost in the mustache he was attempting to grow, to the amusement of his brothers. "It just melts right off."

"You can break the hair if you're rough with it when it's frozen," Carina cautioned. "But you just have to dip your head in to thaw it." She demonstrated, tipping her head back down into the water and emerging with wet hair streaming down her shoulders.

Tania realized that although her body was blazing hot, her ears were actually quite cold, and she slowly eased herself back into the warm water until only her face was out.

The sounds went away when her ears went underwater,

and she lay back and stared up into a golden, pastel sky through hazy steam. She could hear, barely, that the others were continuing to talk, but none of the words could penetrate the water around her.

And then, one did.

Come.

It was a woman's voice, but not Carina's, and Tania shivered at the power in it and nearly dunked herself under. She pulled herself back into an upright position, into the conversation that had continued without her, and looked around.

Carina and Toren were discussing dinner, Rian interjecting once in a while. None of them seemed to have heard the voice and when Tania squinted through the fog, she couldn't see anyone else around them.

"What's up there?" she asked, pointing up a tiny, narrow footpath that came up out of the water and wound away around some of the tall rocks that ringed the pool.

Carina shrugged, but Rian and Toren looked surprised. "It's open?" Toren said.

"I can't remember the last time we were invited," Rian said, shaking his head.

"Invited?" Carina pried. "Invited by who? Invited where?"

"Those are the pools that are technically reserved for royalty," Toren explained. "But even we aren't always allowed."

"Allowed by *who?*" Carina begged.

"Angel," Rian said. "The hot springs spirit. Usually there's a sign warning people away, if you can even see the path at all."

"A spirit?" Tania exclaimed in surprise. "Like a *ghost?*"

"More like a naiad," Rian said, looking up the path. "An elemental fae. She controls the waters."

Carina didn't look nearly as shocked as Tania felt. "Oh, wait, I heard about her!"

Why wouldn't there be spirits, Tania thought wryly. There were shifters and spells and dragons.

She tried not to feel left out and in the dark as Carina eagerly and athletically scrambled out of the hot springs to follow the narrow little path. Even standing with only her shoulders out of the water made her feel chilled, and she wondered how icy the trail was, and whether she should even attempt it. Toren followed Carina, and Rian, halfway out, turned to offer Tania a hand.

Before she could decide if she really wanted to try navigating a hazardous path in bitter cold wearing nothing but her swimsuit, a rush of water cradled her and pushed her right at him. She was half-lifted from the pool so that if she hadn't scrambled up with Rian, she would have been flattened against the rocks.

She thought she heard faint laughter when she turned to look behind her, and there was a strange swirl in the fog.

"You okay?" Rian asked quietly, and Tania turned back to nod. He didn't comment on the water, and it didn't splash against the rocks the way that Tania had expected it to.

Shivering, they followed the winding path up and up, a gorgeous view of snow-covered hills rising in every direction around them. Carina and Toren were both splashing into the pool before they got there and Tania was starting to feel desperately chilled.

The far edge of the water was invisible in the steam. Just as Tania was wondering if it was the same temperature as the other, Toren volunteered, "This pool is usually too hot for humans. Angel must have turned it down for you."

"We sometimes soak in dragon form here," Rian said,

clearly trying not to hover as Tania sat down and slipped into the water. There were no steps here, and she wondered if she would have to let Rian lift her out when they left.

"This one *is* hotter," Carina warned, as Tania dipped her legs in, but it didn't actually feel much warmer than the pool below.

She wasn't sure how deep it would be, so she let go of the edge carefully, and found that there was a bench carved into the stone under the water, just deep enough that they were submerged to their necks. Beyond that, she couldn't touch the bottom with her feet. The far side of the pool was invisible in the steam, and it seemed as if they were somewhere else entirely, with just patches of sky and mountain briefly visible.

Rather suddenly, there was another figure sitting with them, between Carina and Tania.

"Oh!" Tania said, startled, and she backed directly into Rian, sitting next to her. For just a moment, the feel of his skin against hers, his hands touching her reflexively, was more important than the stranger.

"Hi!" Carina said eagerly. "You must be Angel."

Angel leaned back, grinning, but didn't answer as Tania and Rian adjusted so that they were just a few inches apart.

She would be tall, Tania guessed, and her neck was elegant. Her hair was long and dark, but it was hard to tell what color. Her skin was pale and cool, and her eyes, when she turned to look at Tania, were...unexpectedly normal blue eyes, friendly and playful.

Tania found herself smiling back automatically.

"You're starting to come together," Angel said cryptically.

Carina's expression, past Angel, was mystified through the fog. "Who's coming together, now?"

"The queens," Angel said, as if it was obvious.

"You mean, me and Tania?" Carina said in surprise. "The princes' *mates?*"

"Wait," Tania noticed. "What do you mean *starting* to come together? Why would the Compact call more than one queen? Should we expect more of them? How many?"

Angel slid even further into the water, so that her nose was barely above the surface, and her eyes crinkled with amusement.

"Do you know about the Compact?" Rian asked suspiciously.

Angel squirted a stream of water from her mouth as she rose again. "I know the Compact," she said, a teasing smile on her face.

"Can you answer questions about it?" Tania asked, trying to decide if Angel's dark hair was dry or wet.

"I was here when it was made," Angel said. "But it has its own answers."

Past Carina, Toren groaned. "She's like that," he warned, splashing in Angel's direction. "We've been asking questions. Quit being mysterious." He seemed unruffled by the idea that they were sharing the pool with a *spirit* with the power to boil them alive.

Of course, he *was* a dragon prince.

"You aren't asking it the right questions," Angel said, giving Toren a splash in return.

"What are the right questions?" Tania asked.

Angel turned and looked at her and Tania wondered how she had ever thought that the naiad's eyes were normal. They were shining in the fading light, impossibly bright. "Start with the *answer* you want," she said merrily.

Then, as swiftly as she'd appeared, she was gone again, in a swirl of fog and a lingering laugh.

There was a moment of silence, then Toren sighed. "So, that was Angel. She's like that."

"Are there many spirits like this?" Tania asked, peering through the steam.

"They aren't that common," Rian said.

"There's one at the castle, supposedly," Carina said. "I haven't seen it yet. This is the first time I've seen one. I'm a little freaked out."

"What kind of spirit is the one at the castle?" Tania asked, shallowly glad there was *something* that Carina was new at, too. "Another water naiad?"

"No one's really sure," Toren said. He was holding Carina easily in the circle of his arms and just watching them only made Tania more aware of Rian, close but not touching. "Some people see an old woman, some see an old man, some see a dragon, but faded, like a ghost."

Tania startled. "Oh, I saw an old woman." Everyone stared at her. "I mean, I thought she was just someone who worked there, but the guards didn't seem to notice her, and...she spoke oddly. And disappeared."

Carina looked a little jealous now. "You know, I spent an entire night lurking around the west wing hoping I'd meet her. She's supposed to give words of wisdom, did she say anything?"

Tania struggled to remember. Sometimes her recall got uncertain with drugs or pain, but this felt more like a deliberate hole in her memory. "She...she said that...broken things were sometimes stronger."

"What did she look like?" Toren asked. "I once saw an old woman in a white flowing dress. I always wondered if she wasn't the ghost of an ancestor, but no one has been able to figure out who she might be."

"I...don't remember," Tania said, frowning. "It was like...like I wasn't supposed to notice her. Like I couldn't quite *look* at her. It was weird."

Rian made a small noise. "Wait, I saw her once, too, and it was just like that, like I couldn't quite *look*."

"You never told me that!" Toren protested. "What did she tell you?"

"It's hard to remember, but she said...to get out of the way."

"Spirits," Toren scoffed in disgust. Then he swiftly added, "No offense, Angel."

"I'm overheating," Carina said, hauling herself up to sit on the ledge. The water was hot enough that there was no ice immediately around the pool and Carina's face was red. "How can you stand it, Tania?"

Tania looked up at Carina in surprise. "It's very comfortable!"

Toren rose out of the water next to Carina, splashing hot water over the rocks. "Are you feeling weak?" he teased her. "Am I going to have to carry you out again?"

Carina leaned down into the pool to splash him. "Let's go down to the lower pool," she said, climbing easily to her feet. Toren willingly followed, and Tania was alone with Rian again.

It seemed weird to stay so near him now that they had the pool to themselves. Tania moved a little ways away, and it was easier to turn and look at him.

That wasn't much less unsettling than knowing he was close behind her. He was so *gorgeous*, and the broad expanse of his chest was nothing short of amazing.

"Will you...will you show me?" she asked, tentatively.

For a moment, he didn't understand what she was asking, and she watched desire and hope rise in his face.

She didn't want to crush him, but swiftly added, "You said you soak here as a dragon. Can I see it? Him? Them?"

"He doesn't really care about pronouns," Rian said, schooling his face to hide his disappointment, but not fast enough that Tania missed it. "But *him* works."

The space she'd given him was clearly not enough, and Rian pushed away from the edge of the pool and floated out into the water. Tania had to fight down her instinctive urge to follow him, and was glad that she did when, almost invisible through the steam, he shifted.

A great wave heaved towards her as he suddenly displaced a huge volume of water, and Tania had to scramble up the side of the pool trying in vain to keep her head above it. She closed her eyes as it swept over her, and when she opened them, sputtering, Rian was a dragon.

His head was high in the air above her, looking down, and the thick steam gave it all an air of enchantment, as if the improbable view of a dragon were not enough.

His skin—hide?—scales?—were dazzling in the weak light, reflecting in a hundred rainbow colors over a base of coppery-gold. A long neck snaked down into the water, and a spine ridge arched above the surface, huge wings like solar sails from a science fiction novel were folding at his sides.

No, not like solar sails, but not entirely like the bat wings she was expecting, either; Tania found herself running over dragon descriptions from books in her mind and finding that all of them fell short. He was as graceful as any swan, as powerful as any creature that had ever walked the earth, less like a lizard and more like...no, an insect certainly wasn't right, either.

Judging his size by what she could see, Tania realized that the pool must be many, many meters deep, and she was glad she had not known that when she got in.

The long, tapered nose came down out of the mist to her and Tania reached up a wondering hand.

He was warm to the touch and softer than she expected, not rough, exactly, but definitely textured. He sank slowly into the water until only the top of his head was showing, gleaming eyes just above the surface, nostrils submerged. The water swelled up again, more controlled, and spilled over the edges of the rocks.

"You're beautiful," Tania said reverently, her hand still resting on his nose.

Rian blew gently and a riot of bubbles rose from beneath them.

She couldn't help giggling. "You're better than a Jacuzzi."

21

*We **are** better than a Jacuzzi,* Rian's dragon said smugly.

The awe in Tania's eyes was gratifying, and Rian barely kept himself from rising out of the water and spreading his wings to show the rest of his dragon form.

Instead, he shifted. The water sucked into the space that he'd abandoned, and Tania was rather suddenly sitting exposed on the bench at the edge of the pool, clinging to the side. He was more than an arm's length away, his human form near the place his dragon's center of mass had been, and he floated lazily back to her as the water slowly rose again, fed by the springs beneath them.

He pulled himself back up on the ledge, not completely oblivious to the way that she watched him and pretended not to.

"Thank you," she said shyly.

"Does it seem more real, now?"

Tania's dark eyes searched his. "It's all very improbable," she said softly. "But it's hard to deny when I'm sitting in a hot spring with a dragon."

The water was back to their waists now, and Rian was trying to decide how close he could politely sit next to her, and whether he dared to kiss her. She was flushed from the heat, and her eyes were bright and full of...invitation?

As he was trying to work up how to ask, a voice from below split through the fog.

"Hey, Rian! Dinner's in twenty minutes! Quit making out and get down to the restaurant!"

Tania's flush heightened, more apparent on her bare chest than on her cheeks.

"Sorry," Rian said, wishing that Toren was in reach so he could strangle him with his bare hands. "My brother's a tool. Are you hungry?"

"I'm starving," Tania admitted.

He helped her out of the pool and walked nervously behind her as she trekked carefully back down the path. It was somehow not as icy as it had been on the trip up, and they were back at the lower pool in no time.

They had to wade across it to come out on the ramp by the locker rooms, and Rian reluctantly let her go. He took a swift shower and dressed quickly, so that he was waiting in the lobby when Carina and Tania came out, giggling together.

Toren took the longest, and the four of them walked together to the restaurant. They were served in the private hall, a dinner of several decadent courses, and the conversation was light and cheerful.

"It's so nice having another princess to commiserate with," Carina said. "Or...not a princess yet. Me, either, yet. Technically."

"Why *are* there two mates?" Toren asked, as their dinner plates were picked up and the dessert—slices of chocolate cake covered in out-of-season strawberries. "I mean, I know I was kind of *hoping*, because I really didn't want to be a king, but I wasn't sure it was really possible…"

"That's just the first question," Rian said. "Which one is meant to represent us at the Compact Renewal? Which one of us has to be king?"

"Has there ever been more than one mate before?" Carina asked. "Maybe this is just a thing that sometimes happens and you draw straws or something?"

Tania answered with authority, "Never, not in any kingdom." She looked up from her cake as if she realized she'd said it more strongly than they were expecting. "I did my thesis on the Compact. It involved a lot of dry side-research, and at one point I could recite who attended each Renewal, going back four hundred years. Each kingdom had one king and one queen, there was never mention of more. It was almost always the oldest son and his mate."

"So who do we send?"

Silence met Carina's question. No one seemed to be wondering *if* Tania was going to marry Rian. Not even Tania. Which wasn't the same as a *yes*.

"Age before beauty?" Toren joked.

"I guess that's what we have to find out," Rian said, ignoring him. "We brought the Compact with us, I was thinking we'd have some time to look over it while we were here."

"You really just don't know how to have fun, do you?" Toren needled him.

Tania made a disapproving noise, like she wanted to defend him but didn't know how.

"I have plenty of fun," Rian deadpanned. "Yesterday I looked at tax documents in great detail and found an absolutely hilarious reference to *dead assets* in the inheritance section."

Toren groaned. "You could not be more boring if you tried."

"I don't know," Rian retorted, settling his glasses deliberately on his nose. "I could try."

Tania and Carina both laughed, and they polished off their plates.

"Coffee?" the server offered.

"Decaf?" Carina countered. "I plan to sleep like the dead after that soak."

They shared a pot, but didn't linger over it, all of them clearly thinking about succession and duty while they talked of other things. Finally, Toren yawned dramatically. Rian was pretty sure that it was an act and he was less tired and more interested in retiring with his mate.

"Shall we call it a night?" Rian suggested.

Carina and Toren both agreed with embarrassing eagerness and Rian helped Tania into her coat.

"I'm sorry it was all so serious," Rian said, falling into step beside Tania as Carina and Toren scampered ahead for the warm lodge. "I really *was* hoping we could *relax* a little here and have fun."

Tania looked up at him and smiled. "It's been lovely," she assured him quietly. She pulled the collar of her coat up and shivered, then suddenly she clutched Rian's arm and pointed upward.

They were far enough from the springs now that the swirling steam had cleared and they had a view of the dark sky, sparkling with stars and streaked with...

"Northern lights!"

Rian was torn between watching the aurora, dancing in brilliant green streaks above them, or watching Tania, her face aglow with delight.

"They're so...swirly!"

Photos couldn't truly capture how unreal the lights

could be, with their shifting colors and fading edges, looping and swimming in a full arc overhead. They lit up the few drifting clouds, and swam in huge, mesmerizing strands that dissolved and reappeared like…

"It's like magic," Tania breathed, clinging to him for balance as she craned her neck up to watch the show above. "Look at them *dance!*"

It gave them quite an exhibition, dancing in shimmering green waves, edged at times in bright purple and red.

"Those colors are rare," Rian pointed out. "It's usually just pale greens. You're getting a treat!"

They watched until Tania was shivering at his side and Rian could feel her tensing in discomfort. "We should go in," he said reluctantly, not wanting to tear her from the display. "I don't want you to lose all the good work of the springs."

"Yes," she agreed through chattering teeth.

They hurried into the lodge, past more guards than Rian usually saw here, and up the stairs to their rooms. There were more guards at the end of the corridor.

"I'm just down the hall," he said, standing reluctantly in front of Tania's room. "If you…need anything…"

She was still shivering, her eyes bright and her cheeks flushed. "Thank you…" she murmured, and Rian wanted badly to kiss her but knew how hard it would be stop there…and she hadn't said yes to *whatever*.

He laid a swift kiss on her forehead and fled to his own room before he could do something he might not regret.

22

Tania brushed her teeth and changed into a pair of soft leggings and a tank top. She opened her book no less than four times and put it down each time, unread.

She paced her room, restless, her mind full of Rian. His mesmerizing body, his dear expressions, his perfect courtesy. The way he felt, the way he spoke, the way he watched her and always seemed ready to help but equally willing to let her do things herself.

He could be *hers*. It was a dizzying realization, as impossible as dragons and magic and mates. He was waiting on her. All she had to do was say *yes*.

It was hard to remember why she *wasn't* saying yes. What girl didn't want a handsome prince who was willing to lay the keys to his kingdom at her feet?

Tania paced to the closet, where someone had unpacked her clothing and...possibly even ironed it. She picked out a blouse, buttoning it on carefully, and then went out into the hallway. She glanced defiantly at the guards at each end of the hall, steeled herself, and walked to Rian's door.

For a long moment, she stood with her hand raised, not daring to let knuckle touch wood.

What was she *thinking*? Did she really plan on knocking on the door of a prince?

Weirder still, was she honestly planning not to return to her own room for the night?

Why not? Carina had asked her.

Tania was uncomfortably aware of the bland-faced guards at each end of the hall. She was more uncomfortably aware of her own body. For once, it wasn't in pain; all of the stress in her muscles had been leached blissfully away. The only tension left was low in her core, a desperate craving for touch, a hunger, a yearning.

It didn't feel like magic. It felt like she was missing a body part, like she was looking for her last puzzle piece.

Maybe that *was* magic. What did *she* know?

Her hand wavered, brushing the door without sound, but it was enough to spur her to a real knock, and then a second, louder, before she lost her nerve.

The door opened in a rush, like Rian had known she was there and was only waiting for her to be sure.

He was dressed in embroidered silk pajamas, because he was a prince, but Tania only had eyes for his face, for the hopeful, hungry expression in his beautiful, silvery eyes, for the way his mouth worked without words, for the set of his jaw.

"Are you…?"

"Yes," she said breathlessly. "Yes."

Then he was closing the space between them to take her face in his hands and kiss her, and wasn't the chaste promise of a kiss on her forehead that she'd come to expect most nights when they parted, it was a desperate kiss, trembling with need...

He wasn't trembling, she realized, she was the one shaking, and her arms were slipping up around his neck and she was kissing him back and twining herself against him and he felt amazing, all along the length of her, and she couldn't remember a time when her body felt so much like her own as it did when he was touching it.

"Tania," he growled, pulling away from her mouth. "*Titania...*"

They were still in the hallway, surely giving the guards a hell of a show, but Tania didn't care.

"I pray thee, gentle mortal, sing again..." she couldn't resist saying.

Rian chuckled. "Are you calling me an ass, fairy queen?"

"If we shadows have offended..." Tania teased.

He made a little sound of delight and pulled her close again, and they staggered together into the bedroom, a tangle of desperate touches and lingering kisses.

She made a noise of surprise when the bed struck the backs of her legs, and Rian pulled away in concern. "Did I hurt you?" he asked.

"No!" Tania said quickly. She didn't think he *could.*

But the tenor of their lovemaking had changed. Rian went from desperate to deliberate, picking her gently up and laying her back onto his bed so easily she might have weighed nothing. He kissed her forehead—a sweet, gentle kiss—then kissed her nose, and when she whimpered and tipped her head back, kissed her exposed throat, so softly and tenderly that it felt like feathers.

He undressed her slowly, caressing every piece of skin as he exposed it, slipping buttons from holes so carefully that

Tania wanted to squirm but kept herself still until her blouse had been unbuttoned to the bottom. He undid her cuffs next, like it was a ritual, and pulled her up into a seated position. She stroked his arms and his chest; the silk was mesmerizing over the body she'd been trying not to fantasize about for so long.

"*Northernbookwyrm*," she murmured, and she had to giggle.

"*T.perez*," he whispered back, and then he was kissing her again, and they were wriggling out of all their remaining clothing with new urgency.

Everything was soft and hard. Soft hair, hard muscle, soft noises, hard cock brushing her leg. Tania dared to touch it, softly, and Rian's hands spasmed on her shoulders.

"Sorry…" he hissed, releasing her, and Tania moved until it wasn't her leg that it was touching.

For a moment, they held there, touching close, but not pressing. Then Tania, feeling like she was at a fever pitch, reached up and took his bottom lip in her teeth, as gently as possible.

He slid into her slowly, filling deeper and thicker, until Tania thought she could surely take no more. She released his lip with a cry of pleasure, and he backed off a fraction then filled her even further. Tania could not have said when they began moving together in earnest, frantic and fierce.

Her world seemed to explode in light and sensation, and Rian was her safety and her shelter and her north star, taking her to places of pleasure she had never imagined.

23

Rian lay in the afterglow, curled with Tania and feeling unmistakably on top of the world.

They were so *good* together.

He'd been able to give her every thrill he'd hoped, too, raised her to a fever pitch and set her free. His own release had almost been an afterthought. The joy in her face, her soft cries, the beauty of her body's reception to his touch...

"Did I...hurt you?" he had to ask.

She stirred, and Rian had to stop himself from holding on tighter.

"No," she said, and she turned in his arms to smile up at him as he propped up on one elbow to gaze down at her. "I'm sore, and it will be worse in the morning, but it was entirely worth it."

Rian felt a swell of pride. "I love you," he blurted. "Will you marry me?"

The room was poorly lit; Rian had been reading on a tablet in night mode and preparing for just another lonely night of restless sleep when he first became aware of Tania at his door.

But the expression of alarm that flashed over Tania's face was as unmistakable as if her face had been in sunlight and Rian desperately wished he could take his words back.

"I'm sorry," he said swiftly. "You don't have to answer." He was such a *clod*.

Her face softened at once, but it settled into something more sorrow than satisfaction. "I...care a lot for you, Rian," she said gently. "You're probably my best friend, and I've had a crush on you since you got my obscure Tolkein reference in one of our earliest emails. Even before I saw your naked Internet photos. But...*marriage*. You know what that means. This isn't a courthouse, spur-of-the-moment, officiated-by-Elvis thing. You're asking…"

"I know," Rian said gravely. "I come with a lot of baggage."

"So do I," Tania pointed out, sitting up to gaze at him with dark, soulful eyes. "I can't always even walk under my own power. And you're asking me to add the weight of a crown. A tiara at least. That's...a lot."

"Too much," Rian said. "I'm sorry to ask."

"Are you cursed to ask me, night after night, until the spell is broken?" Tania teased gently.

Rian chuckled. "Sometimes it seems like it," he admitted. "Can you ever learn to love a beast?"

Tania's mouth curved into a knowing smile. "Will you share your library full of books that haven't been written yet?"

Even reminding himself that he was taking it too far couldn't stop Rian from replying truthfully, "I would give you everything I have, everything I am, everything I ever will be."

She looked at him as if she could taste the truth in the

air between them, with eyes a little brighter than they should be.

"Is this the spell?" she asked plaintively. "Is it just magic that makes me feel this way?" She touched his face, brushing a lock of hair over his ear and lingering with her fingers there.

"This isn't the spell," Rian said, shivering under the touch of her fingers. "Spells don't *last*."

"It doesn't *feel* faded," Tania said, so quietly that Rian would not have heard her if they had not been almost nose to nose. She had not taken her hand back, so Rian turned his head and kissed her palm.

Her breath hissed in, and Rian would have turned and laid her back down on the bed to make love to her again if he had not learned to recognize the tenor of the noise. "You're hurting."

Tania gave a hiccup of a laugh. "Is *that* the spell?"

"No," Rian said firmly. "I just know you a little now. What do you need?"

Tania rolled her shoulders experimentally. "I should take a muscle relaxer before bed," she decided.

"I'll get it for you," Rian said, putting a kiss on her forehead. "Where will I find it?"

Tania gave him her key and described her makeup kit. "I call it a makeup kit," she chuckled. "But it's ninety percent drugs, one tube of lipstick, and a handful of flossers."

Rian pulled on his pajama pants, not bothering with anything else. "I'll be back in a blink. You want something to take them with from the vending machine?"

"Water is fine," she assured him.

He took the ice bucket with him.

He felt a little like a thief, unlocking her room with the guards pretending not to notice him or the fact that he wasn't wearing a shirt. The makeup kit was on the counter in the bathroom right off the hallway door, but three of the pill bottles were sitting beside it.

Rian was still figuring out how to Tetris them into the overstuffed makeup kit when he heard something deeper in the room and he and his dragon were both suddenly on high alert.

Danger! Magic! his dragon warned.

He abandoned the kit and picked up the ice bucket, walking quietly to the door of the bathroom to peer out carefully into the room.

At first, there was nothing, just a crackling sound in an empty space by the foot of the bed.

Then, as Rian watched in astonishment, there was suddenly a rift split out of nowhere and a shadowy figure was standing before him, lit from behind. He was blinking into a strange, bright room. Sunlight was streaming through windows beyond, and there were words written all over the floor. He was too surprised to move at first, and the figure stepped into Tania's room.

Rian's dragon roared in outrage and he nearly shifted, but realized at the last moment that he would destroy a good part of the lodge if he did so. Instead, he hurled his ice bucket at the person and charged forward with a wild yell.

His hand closed around an arm and he caught the interloper with his other fist flailing. It was a lucky grab and an unlucky hit, just glancing from the...woman? The hair was long, but the figure wrenched from his grip with more strength than he was expecting and retreated. There were exclamations from the other place, someone shouted, *"Alto!"* and the rift snapped shut with a crackle of energy and a scream that stopped abruptly with a snap.

The dented lid to the ice bucket and two partial fingers,

severed diagonally just past the second knuckle, were the only sign that anything out of the normal had happened there.

Rian stood there a long moment, heart hammering in his chest, staring down at the blood seeping into the hotel carpet.

Someone had invested the time and power into a portal spell, to come here. To *Tania's* room. After her? After... Rian looked past the bed to the desk where a leather briefcase lay. The briefcase with the pages of the Compact.

He wasn't sure what was worse, the idea that someone knew they'd been brought here, that someone might be after Tania, or the possibility that he might not have been able to keep her safe if she had simply come back to her room to sleep. Just as he recognized the adrenaline and anger surging through him, there was a pounding on the door behind him. "Your Highness?"

Rian nearly took the door off the hinges answering it, and was pushing through the guards before they could even react, flying back down the hall to his own room.

Tania looked up in alarm at his entrance, but didn't make a sound of protest as Rian gathered her into his arms and held her until his trembling had passed. She had put on a bathrobe, and he could feel the tension in her through the terrycloth.

"What happened?" she asked, when he could finally let her go.

"Someone broke into your room," he said, not entirely sure that she was safe. "Probably the same woman who made an attempt on the vault last week." He prowled the room, listening for the crackling sound that had first alerted him. Outside the open door, in the hallway, the guards had called for backup, and there was a swirl of voices and commotion.

Tania blinked. "The Compact?"

"I didn't give her time to find what she was looking for," Rian said, still not sure if Tania had been the target, or the pages. He went to shut the door to the hallway, a quick glance showing that more guards had already arrived. He heard Captain Luke calling orders from Tania's room.

"Was anyone hurt?" Tania looked anxiously out towards the noisy hall as Rian shut the door.

Rian thought about the fingers he'd left behind on the floor. "No one who matters," he said grimly.

He returned to Tania, still sitting at the edge of the bed.

"Rian, Rian, what happened?" Toren pounded on the door and tested the locked handle.

Rian rose to open it for him; the door wouldn't stand long against dragon strength. "Coming!"

"Captain Luke said there was a portal in Tania's room!"

"A *portal!*" Tania cried.

Carina was behind Toren, wrapped in a bathrobe bearing the resort logo. "I thought you said that portals would be a one-time thing, that they were too complicated and energy-consuming to use twice! Tania, are you okay?"

"I'm fine," Tania said, tightening her own bathrobe around her. "I...wasn't there."

A moment of amused silence met her shy statement. Toren elbowed Rian approvingly in the ribs and grinned at him.

"Were they after *Tania?*" Toren wanted to know then, and the mood in the room sobered abruptly. He put an arm around Carina protectively.

If Rian had been closer to Tania, he would have done the same. "Either her, or the Compact," he said grimly.

From the doorway, Captain Luke cleared her throat. "Did you get a good look at the owner of these fingers?" she asked.

"Not really," Rian said, shaking his head. "She was lit from behind, full daylight through big windows. No, not full daylight—I could see the sun at the top of the windows." He gestured with his arm to show the angle.

"That narrows down the timezone," Toren pointed out.

"Majorca is early evening right now," Luke said thoughtfully. "Tell me what happened, everything you can remember."

She didn't take notes, but Rian could watch her cataloging the details as he described the crackling portal and the assailant. "There were others, on the opposite side," he said thoughtfully. "I didn't see them, but I heard more voices."

Luke frowned. "Report anything else that you remember," she growled. "I'm having the perimeter checked; the last portal, they breached the back barrier shortly before the portal was attempted. Raval theorized that they may have some kind of *shortcut* device that allows a portal with less energy."

"This could happen *again?*" Tania squeaked, and Rian closed the distance between at last to put his arms around her.

24

Tania felt helplessly out of place when they returned to the castle, more so than usual. Even Carina, in flannel and striped tights, looked like she was comfortable in what could only be considered a war room, standing confidently near Toren. All of the brothers were wearing the royal uniform, along with a black-haired man that Tania didn't know. She thought for a moment he must be Kenth, the only brother she hadn't met, but he didn't look like any of the others. He looked Mediterranean, possibly older than Fask, and when he grinned at her, he showed bright white teeth, his dark gold eyes sparkling in amusement.

He was also the only one who seemed to notice her at first, and he moved to shake her hand. "You must be the lovely *señorita* Perez. I am Drayger."

It took Tania a moment to recognize the name; he was one of the bastard sons of the Majorcan line. Tania was surprised to find him here, but not terribly surprised when he drew her hand to his mouth to kiss it.

"Drayger," Rian said coolly from her elbow as she took her hand back. "Why are you wearing a royal uniform?"

"Yeah, I thought you were trying to maintain your double agent cover," Toren said, not too subtly moving between the illegitimate Majorcan prince and Carina so he wouldn't offer to kiss her hand as well.

"Sorry, Your Highness," Drayger said to Toren. "It was a good try, but things rarely work out like they do in movies. My...employers...were unconvinced that I was making a go of actually trying to complete the contract, and there were accusations flying. My codes stopped working in the computer system, so I got the information I could and decided that leaving was in the best interests of my skin."

"Just like that," Tray said suspiciously. "And now we're supposed to trust you?"

"He did try to save my life," Carina pointed out.

Drayger blew her a kiss.

"*Try* is the operative word there," Toren pointed out, glaring at him. "And you didn't say why you were wearing one of our uniforms."

Drayger's grin only widened. "Because it irritates the captain of your guard so entirely."

"Be nice," Tray interjected. "Luke is still sore because she didn't catch on to the fact that Shadow was an assassin."

"To be fair," Carina said, "it was hard to take Shadow seriously when he was constantly rolling on his back and licking his own balls." Her voice was complicated, full of grief and guilt, and Tania was sure she was missing some important details to the story. Was Shadow an assassin or a dog?

Tania abruptly remembered shifters, and realized that he must have been both. Her life had gotten very *weird*.

Then Captain Luke herself came sweeping into the room with Fask, and everyone moved towards their chairs.

Rian was seated toward the head of the table, Fask took the seat at the end, with the captain at his right. Tania had to try hard not to stare at her, with her beautiful golden skin and striking chin tattoos almost as arresting as her hard gaze.

The captain was not amused by Drayger's choice of dress; they exchanged a sizzling look before she turned to Fask.

"We have analyzed the fingers that we found, but when we had our caster try to trace them back to source, we were blocked," she announced.

That caused a murmur of speculation.

"That could indicate that we are indeed dealing with another member of the Small Kingdoms," Fask said; he didn't look like he was hearing this news for the first time.

Raval made a low noise. "Or they have blocking spells of their own. We already know they had two portal spells, which by itself is pretty impressive."

Toren looked down the table to Drayger. "Do you think it could be Majorca?"

Drayger spread his fingers as if to prove he had them all. "Could be Majorca. Could be any number of others. My direct employers were very unspecific and claimed no allegiance, and I have no idea if this is related to them or not."

"I doubt we'll have much use for you, going forward," Luke said dismissively, her dislike not the slightest bit masked. "I question why you were invited to this meeting."

"He's offered to answer any questions we have," Fask said quellingly. "And we appreciate his assistance."

Luke ignored both of them and turned icy dark eyes on Rian. "I want to go over the hot springs incursion again.

You said that there were multiple people on the other side of the portal."

"I didn't see any of them," Rian said apologetically. "I threw the ice bucket at the nearest one, and tried to tackle them. There were some voices, one of them shouted, and then the portal closed."

"What did they shout?" Raval asked from down the table. Raval was the caster, Tania remembered.

Rian frowned. "Allo...Aldo..."

"*Alto*," Tania guessed suddenly, just as Drayger, sitting two chairs further down the table, said the same.

"Spanish for *halt*, or *stop*," he explained, before Tania could.

"They speak Spanish in Majorca," Luke pointed out, ignoring Drayger to speak to Rian. "And the daylight you saw matches their timezone."

They talked about all the details Rian could remember: the marks on the floor, the decor, how many people he thought there might have been, the features of the unknown assailant…

Suddenly Rian snapped his fingers. "You couldn't trace the fingers because they weren't ours, but doesn't the Compact allow tracking of our *own* property?"

Everyone looked down the table at Raval, who shrugged. "It ought to. Why, did you tag him with something?"

"I threw the ice bucket at him," Rian reminded him. "Only the lid remained behind."

Raval nodded slowly. "Yeah, we ought to be able to trace that. I don't know if it would be enough to prove anything, though. And they may have gotten rid of it."

"It would still be nice to *know*," Fask said firmly, looking pleased. "Captain, if you would have the caster of the guard do that?"

Luke nodded crisply. "We collected the lid with the other evidence. I'll put Officer Prang on it as soon as we break."

Tania found herself wondering why the caster hadn't attended the meeting; surely they would be more useful here than she would.

Then the topic changed to Toren and Carina's forthcoming wedding, and *succession*, and she *really* wanted to be anywhere else.

"Are we officially announcing another engagement?" Fask asked pointedly. At least he didn't ask *when* they would be announcing it like it was a foregone conclusion.

"No," Rian said quickly, moving slightly as if he could protect Tania with his body.

"Why not?" Drayger asked bluntly. "If the Compact has tapped her, there's no real point in putting it off."

"What about Carina?" Fask pointed out, ignoring Drayger. "Has she been...un-tapped? Who do we send to the Renewal?"

"Tania and Rian can go," Carina volunteered quickly, grinning across the table at Tania.

Tania smiled ruefully back. "Oh no, I insist," she said wryly back. "You were here first."

"I have to think there was a *reason* that Tania was called," Fask said grimly. "And not all of the possible reasons are pleasant to consider."

The table was silent for a moment, and Tania caught the look of worry that flashed over Carina's face.

"The Compact runs ahead," Tania observed. "It anticipates needs." Like a need for a second mate, if the first was lost.

She said it too quietly for Fask to hear, but Rian and Raval both looked at her solemnly. Across the table, Carina and Toren were talking about what needed to happen before the wedding, and how it might conflict with a second engagement announcement.

Runs ahead. Anticipates…

Tania felt like she was on the verge of a thought, escaping fast like a dream.

"Oh," she said suddenly, and then everyone did turn and look at her because she said it much louder than she meant to. "Oh!" she repeated. "Do you remember what Angel said?"

"Angel says a lot of mysterious nonsense," Toren scoffed.

"She said to start with the *answer* we *want*."

"What's the answer we want?" Carina asked. "I honestly don't want to be queen."

Tania looked around the table. "You all want Fask to be king, right?"

"Yes," Toren agreed without hesitation.

"Absolutely," Rian added. "But…"

"So the question we need to ask isn't *which one of **us** has to be queen*, it's *how do we find Fask **his** mate*?"

Everyone was silent, staring at Fask, who looked solemnly back at each of them in turn. Then Rian said slowly, "Raval did say there might be a way to…activate a mate."

Raval shrugged. "I couldn't find anything useful."

Tania stood up and boldly reached for the copy of the Compact sitting in the middle of the table.

"That part here…" Tania flipped over a few of the pages. "Where they talk about treaties and the alliance *across borders*." She stabbed a finger at one of the lines. "Clause seventeen. *Should two Kingdoms choose, the first fruit of each line may act as conduit and may, by choice before call, pledge by the twenty-first section in order to resolve a confusion.* This probably qualifies as a confusion."

"What does that even mean?" groaned Toren. "What's the twenty-first section?"

"I don't know," Tania confessed. "It's all in clauses and parts. I never saw a twenty-first *section.*"

"I thought that was for *treaty* disputes, not succession," Raval said. "I always figured it was referring to mediation between oldest children when their parents couldn't agree. And there's nothing about mates there."

"Not here," Tania admitted. "But later, in clause thirty, it uses that same language but reversed, call before choice, in that whole section about mates. So it stands to reason that it's talking about the same thing."

Carina scowled. "I can't say I like that *no choice* wording about mates."

Tania hissed thoughtfully. "It's not saying no choice...exactly. It says a call *before* choice. Not *preference to*, but in *advance* of." The Compact ran *ahead*.

Carina blinked at her and they exchanged a long look that Tania wasn't entirely sure how to interpret. Then she smiled and said, "Huh."

Tania was sharply aware of Rian, at her side. She could reach out and touch him, if she wanted to, and she rather desperately did. Was that what *he* was feeling? What *she* was feeling? What she was *going* to feel? It didn't have that same overwhelming, tumbling feeling of too much at once, too much to sort out that it had before.

She just...really wanted him, wanted to be at his side, couldn't imagine not having him near.

"Could section twenty-one have been stolen?" Rian suddenly suggested, and everyone was quiet as they considered the terrible idea. "*Has* the Compact been altered?"

"I don't *remember* a section twenty-one," Tania confessed. "But I don't entirely understand how all of this works."

"If they've got portals," Raval growled, "then they've been working on this a long while. Perhaps this goes back further than we know."

"Leinani," Fask said, speaking as suddenly as Rian had.

"Who?" Drayger was one bag of popcorn from an utterly irreverent audience.

The rest of the table, except for Carina and Tania, made noises of speculation.

"I'm with Drayger on this; who's Leinani?" Carina asked.

"Oldest child of the Mo'orea sovereigns. She's...what, sixteen?" Toren answered.

"She's twenty," Fask said slowly. "But she'd be twenty-one well before the Renewal."

Mo'orea. Alaska's closest ally. It was a beautiful solution.

"You're not *that* much older," Toren pointed out. "There was more of an age difference between mother and father."

"But she was human. Leinani is a dragon, too," Tray pointed out.

"Have you met her?" Carina asked Fask cautiously.

Fask nodded. "A few years ago," he said. "A big diplomatic thing on the island. She visited here once as a child before that, must have been ten years ago."

"I remember her being really shy," Raval said. "We all tried to get out of entertaining her."

"She didn't have any use for a bunch of noisy boys," Toren recalled. "Kind of a girly girl. I think Tray put a woodfrog down the back of her dress and made her cry."

Tray chuckled. "I'd forgotten about that."

Tania tapped the pages of the copy neatly together as she re-stacked them, and realized that Fask was watching her, not the others.

"Do you think you could figure out how to make her my mate...supposing Mo'orea is willing? Supposing *Leinani* is okay with it?"

Tania stared back at him and licked her lips. "I never looked at it from that angle before. Even just thinking about magic as real is pretty new to me. But I have some ideas."

Fask's eyes, silvery like Rian's, seemed to drill into her. "I'd like you to make this your focus. Maybe the Compact called you here for a *different* reason. Maybe you aren't intended to be Rian's..."

"She's my *mate*," Rian snarled.

Tania didn't need a magic bond to recognize that he was feeling protective and angry, and she put her hand on his arm without thinking about it, squeezing in...warning? To let him know...

She took her hand back abruptly, overwhelmed by sudden realization.

"No one is saying she isn't," Fask said diplomatically.

"Down, boy!" Tray teased.

Toren, across the table, only laughed.

Rian didn't look at her, only scowled down at the table in front of him, while Tania wrestled with her own thoughts. She ought to feel relieved by the idea that the magic had a different purpose for her. She ought to feel like she had an escape plan now. Solve the succession problem, and she'd be free.

But she didn't want an escape plan.

She only wanted Rian.

25

Rian didn't have a chance to talk with Tania after the meeting, whisked away instead with Toren and Fask to talk politics and meet with the ruling counsel and brush up on all the obscure diplomatic details he'd never thought he'd need in life.

He corrected their assumption that he and Tania were engaged so many times that the words started to lose their meaning, and they worked right through dinner. He wandered through the kitchen, the Compact in its briefcase at his side, for enough food to get through the night and staggered to his rooms at last.

The guards at his door were a surprise at first, then he felt a surge of anticipation. If they were there, Tania was.

She was sitting in one of the big leather chairs, her legs tucked up beneath her, and when he came quietly in, she looked up and her whole face lit up.

Everything was better when she smiled at him.

He would be the king of Alaska for this woman. Or not, if that was what she wanted. He would give up a crown and move to Florida, if she asked.

He tossed the heavy Compact to the chair beside her and bent to kiss her. He meant to keep it just to a kiss, a simple greeting, a wordless claim, but she reached up and drew him down with the barest caress at each side of his face, the slightest invitation absolutely irresistible.

He only kept himself from pulling her roughly up into his arms by sheer force of will, keeping himself to a gentle touch and a light kiss at her neck before reluctantly pulling away. "What are you reading?" he asked, moving the Compact to sit beside her. His decor had never included a lot of loveseats or couches, and he was beginning to regret that. He would have liked to sit close to her side.

She flushed, and Rian realized that she looked tired. "It's that romance you started reading me on the plane. I tried to look through the legal books you gave me, but my brain was just..." She waved a hand helplessly.

"You don't have to apologize," Rian told her swiftly. "You never have to apologize. I never wanted to trap you in any of this, you have been so strong, and so amazing, and we have asked *so* much of you."

Tears welled up in her eyes. Gratitude, Rian hoped, rather than anything worse.

"Sorry," she said, wiping at them furiously. "I'm sorry."

"We've been so busy," Rian said. "And the hot springs was supposed to be a break and it wasn't, and I'm the one who's sorry."

"I don't want to be trouble," Tania said. "If I hadn't insisted on taking the Compact with us…"

"You aren't trouble," Rian said, unable to bear the arms of the chair between them. He got up, scooped her into his arms, and sat down again, cradling her in his lap. She sighed into his embrace, and he could feel the weariness in her entire body.

"I just don't have the *spoons* to be a queen," Tania said regretfully, cuddling close. "It's so impossible."

For a long moment, Rian just held her. "I'll give you all the spoons I can," he promised. Then he remembered to prod, "The doctor that was recommended…"

"I see him on Tuesday," Tania said. "We've talked on the phone and he's getting my scans from Florida, but I don't want to get too hopeful. I've…tried a lot of things, the last few years."

"Did you like him?" Rian was prepared to fire him on the spot.

"He didn't tell me that I just needed to get more exercise and to stop being *hysterical*, so that was a great first step." It felt like she was damning him with faint praise and Rian's dragon grumbled at the idea that other doctors might ever have dared dismiss her. "It shouldn't take being royalty adjacent to actually get an appointment that takes me seriously," she added with vinegar. "It's just an awful system, and I wish I could change it."

She sat up wearily. "Sometimes, I think maybe that's why *I'm* here. Maybe the Compact chose me because I have some big job to do… Do you think…I'm supposed to foment a social revolution, that I'm supposed to be like Carina and be some kind of champion of justice, that the Compact has some *bigger purpose* with the mates? Maybe *that's* why I'm here. It *shouldn't* take being a prince to get someone help when they need it. I couldn't make a difference as an unemployed librarian in Florida, but maybe I *could* as a queen of Alaska…" Her face fell. "But then, I can't make it through one lousy charity event."

"You don't have to," Rian said fiercely. "You don't have to save the world, you don't have to do more, you don't have to try harder. Tania, you aren't a bad person for taking care of yourself first, of recognizing how much you can do, how many *spoons* you have. Don't you dare take the weight of the world on your shoulders. You *do* enough. You *are* enough. Exactly as you are."

Tania sucked in her breath. "But I…"

Rian touched her nose. "You do *enough*," he repeated. "Don't hold yourself to an impossible standard when you're already so much more than anyone I've ever met."

She smiled reluctantly and sagged back into his arms.

Rian could feel her slowly relax in his arms.

"I wish I knew how to thank you, for everything you've done," she murmured, and Rian held her closer.

Marry me, he almost begged. *Say you'll stay forever.* But he didn't want to be the guy who couldn't take a no.

She is our mate, his dragon reminded him confidently. *Forever is already ours.*

Rian rose to his feet, still holding Tania, and carried her back into the bedroom. His bed had been made at some point; Mrs. James had stepped up the housekeeping service since Tania had arrived.

He kissed her forehead and prepared to tuck her under the covers.

"We were going to brainstorm about how specific alterations to original pages might affect the Compact and identify weak spots," she protested, not releasing him. "And try to figure out what the trigger is for making the mate bond for Fask and what section twenty-one is."

"You should get some sleep," Rian told her firmly. "We'll allot some spoons to it in the morning."

She still didn't let go of him, and one of her hands was making little circles on the back of his neck. "I'm tired," she said. "But I'm not really…sleepy."

It was all the invitation Rian needed to kiss her and tip

her back onto the pillows so he could worship her with his mouth and fingers.

Maybe she hadn't said *yes* to marrying him yet, but he would take *whatever* in the meantime.

26

Sometimes waking up was torture and Tania tried her hardest to stay asleep to escape the pain. But Rian's arms were around her now, the comfortable warmth of his body all along her, and waking up was as lovely as dreaming was.

Her prince.

Her *dragon* prince.

Her *waking* dragon prince. Or at least, certain parts of him were.

Tania squirmed a little, delighted by the feeling of his cock, pressing against her leg through silk pajamas.

Surely it would be worth a late morning and the use of a few spoons to…

Tania became aware of something else, a crackling noise, and a sudden confused fear of fire had her eyelids jerking open in time to see a flash of sudden daylight through the open bedroom door. It was too bright to be early Alaskan morning light; it looked like midday summer sun, and she sat up and reached in panic to Rian. "A portal?!"

He sat bolt upright, growling and scrambling up. "Stay here," he commanded and faster than a man of his size ought to be able to move, he was dashing out of the room into his library...and shutting the door behind him.

Tania fought her way out from beneath the covers with considerably less grace. She paused long enough to pull leggings on under her sleeping shirt and was reaching for her bathrobe when Rian cried out in shock and pain. Tania thought her heart might stop.

Her phone...her phone was out in the library, dammit. Tania picked up her cane, wishing for the first time that she'd picked a heavier model as she hefted it. Then she was at the door, and charging out before she could think because Rian was roaring again.

Tania's entrance had been muffled by the noise of the portal, and Rian's cries, and she had a moment to take in the scene.

A tall woman with long dark hair and a big, scowling, square-faced man were standing before a yawning rip in space that could only be a portal. Tania felt as if she could feel the energy it was taking to keep it open, like there was a weird flatness to the air all around. The woman was shoving papers around on Rian's cluttered desk, and Tania knew what she was going for even before she made a noise of triumph and held the messenger bag with the Compact aloft. There was a page of paper on the floor burning impossibly slowly, and the woman had a bandage over the fingers of one hand.

Rian seemed to be grappling with invisible bonds, moving forward at a molasses speed and raging ineffectively. He seemed unable to speak but made growls of fury.

The woman spotted Tania and gave a cry of alarm, so that the man turned and noticed her. He was holding a handful of papers, and he immediately shuffled through, pulled one out and said something that sounded like nonsense, waving the page at Tania.

Not sure what the spell would do, but sure that it wasn't going to be pleasant, Tania dived awkwardly for cover behind one of Rian's big leather chairs, cursing her clumsiness. Her cane skittered across the floor.

The paper burst into flame and the man dropped it from his fingers as it fell to ash and the chair that Tania was using for cover was suddenly covered with wild purple fur, several inches thick.

The woman shouted in what sounded like Spanish but wasn't quite, clearly berating the man, and he growled back, "How was I to know, Amara?" in English as he pulled out another page.

There was pounding on the door, and shouting in the hallway. Tania drove herself up to her knees and cast around for a weapon, any weapon. Something she could throw… She couldn't let the woman escape with the Compact, whatever else happened. She risked being without cover to crawl back to the bookshelf behind her and snatch up the heaviest book she could reach, hurling it —badly—at the man with the handful of loose spells.

The book went wide and he roared a word that Tania didn't catch, and then had to peel a burning page from his hands before the others caught fire. A green dome of light slowly expanded away from him, and the page lay at his feet, burning fiercely.

"Not that one, fool!" the dark-haired woman—Amara —cried. "You'll block the portal!"

"I don't see you doing better!"

Tania threw another book, and another. None of them hit their targets, but at least they were keeping the thieves occupied. Rian seemed to be fighting free from whatever bonds had held him, and the door to the hallway was being battered by the guards.

She didn't have to take them down, Tania reminded herself. She just had to stall them long enough that someone else could.

With a burst of fear-driven adrenaline, she rose to her feet, scooping up her cane and rushing past Rian, who was moving like heavy weights were attached to every limb, snarling and struggling slowly forward.

He made a wordless sound of protest and alarm as she darted past him, ignoring the ache in her hip and the familiar reluctance of her own limbs.

Cane raised, Tania knew that she had no chance of winning any kind of fight with these people. But the burning pages on the floor...if she could put them out, would that stop the spell? The spells were within the green sphere of light and she hurtled herself at the barrier before she could stop to think.

Pain exploded through her, bright and clear, like every nerve ending in her body had burst into flame. Tania gritted her teeth, and the ache of her jaw was familiar and a welcome distraction. Focus, fight through it. She *knew* how to do that. The last years were all practice for this moment, for this trial. There was a smoldering page at her feet, the one that had trapped Rian. She could not walk, could not force her limbs to obey, in a terrible exaggeration of the trouble she often had, but she could fall, and she fell forward, the cane dropping from her hands.

And the spell did not go out.

It only burned, right through her, in an endless, searing pain that played counter to the agony that the green light was inflicting.

She would not scream. She would not give this man the satisfaction, even if she could not keep him from finding another spell in his haphazard handful. Her jaw was locked so tightly she suddenly worried, with a surprisingly clear area of her brain, that she might crack her own teeth.

Amara was cursing and Tania saw through watering eyes that the green hemisphere of light was still spreading from her partner in crime, between Amara and the portal. She was trying to edge past the green light without letting it touch her, the Compact in her hands like a shield. Tania realized that her cane was inches from her hand and forced her fingers to reach out and close around the shaft.

She flicked it out, hooking Amara's ankle, and yanked as hard as her spasming muscles could manage, pulling her by the foot into the green light she was so desperately trying to avoid.

The scream Amara gave was the stuff of nightmares, and she dropped the messenger bag with the Compact to wrench herself away. The Compact was left inside the pool of light, and Tania could see the deliberation in Amara's eyes as she stared into the space, clearly weighing her options. The ball of pain was still swelling, and it would cover the portal in moments. She glanced at the door, at the Compact, with hatred at Tania, and then she fled back through the portal and shouted *Alto!* as the man cried out in dismay and the portal and the green dome collapsed into nothing behind her.

The burning pages collapsed into cold ash and the pain vanished, leaving Tania feeling hollow and exhausted.

The man was cursing and flipping desperately through the papers in his hands. Did he have another portal spell? Everyone kept saying that it was impossible that they'd had *two* of them, but a third one had clearly brought them here.

He bent to take up the leather bag holding the

Compact and Tania knew she had to do something to stop him and couldn't imagine what that would be.

There was suddenly a shriek of breaking things and Tania could see Rian through her tears, shifting and expanding and crashing through ceiling and walls; his library seemed enormous, but it wasn't meant to contain a dragon. He pounced forward at the man holding the Compact, and pinned him between two legs like tree trunks, lowering a snarling face full of teeth at him as he fell backwards in fear.

The Compact was dropped, and the loose papers the man was holding fell like rain over Tania as she lay, too empty to even blow away the page that fell over her face.

She heard the doors to the library finally burst open. There was a scuffle that she heard rather than saw, because it was too much effort to keep her stinging eyes open.

"Tania? Tania!"

Rian was human again, and drawing her into his worried embrace. Tania wanted to beg him to stop, because everything must still hurt, but it was really only the echo of the awful hurt, and it felt so good to be in his arms where she belonged that she didn't want to fuss. She managed to make a noise that she hoped was reassuring.

"Tania..." he kissed her forehead, pulled her into his lap, cradled her close and she could open her eyes again at last. "Tania, my *love*."

The noise she made at that was somewhat happier. "Yes," she sighed.

"Yes, what?" Rian asked plaintively.

"Just...yes." Tania didn't want to move; her whole body was still in shock over the searing pain and its sudden departure. "Yes to everything. All of it."

Rian kissed her, his chaste kiss to the forehead, but

lingered there, pressing his lips to her hairline and holding her close.

"You can't steal the magic from the world and think you'll get away with it forever!" The guards had secured the square-faced man and were frog-marching him, shouting and struggling out of the room as Captain Luke surveyed the damage. "You'll regret this! We aren't alone!"

"Oh, Rian," Tania managed to say. "Your *library*."

"It doesn't matter," he insisted. "They're just books."

Tania made a noise of protest and wondered if she could sit up yet. She felt weirdly free of pain, but recognized that it was probably only the contrast between what she had been feeling and what she was feeling now.

"Who were they?" she wanted to know.

"We'll find out," Captain Luke assured her. "Do you require medical assistance?"

Tania really could sit up, and she did, though she didn't offer to get out of Rian's lap. "I don't think that I do," she said with some surprise. She experimented with rolling her shoulders and decided that it felt about the same as always. "I'm fine now."

Rian reluctantly let go of her and Captain Luke handed her the cane. With a boost from Rian, she was back on her feet, staring around at the wreckage. There were gaps in the ceiling that were letting swirling cold air in, and Tania had to wince at the carnage of books scattered about—the broken spines and lost pages hurt her librarian soul more than throwing herself around during a magical battle.

Rian gathered up some of the fallen spells as he got to his own feet, frowning at them curiously. "This looks like a child's handwriting," he observed.

Tania peered at the pages. It was untidy, with big, loopy letters, nothing like the perfect lettering of the Compact or the vault door. "It's not the same, either," she pointed out. Each page looked like it had been written by a different person, sloppy and unsteady.

"Raval would have kittens over spells like these," Rian said wryly.

"I'll need to take those for documentation," Captain Luke said, frowning. "I'll want to question our prisoner and meet with you and Fask once I've gotten everything in order. I'll have the staff put tarps over the books until the roof can be repaired."

Neither of them could bear to watch such indignity to his library, so they left Rian's rooms for Tania's below.

"Are you sure you're alright?" Rian asked anxiously, as Tania suddenly halted on the stairs.

She turned and clutched his arm. "We're so blind!" she said.

Rian looked around anxiously. "What do you mean?"

Tania found near-hysterical laughter rising up in her throat. "The Compact. It's literal. Like...*literally* literal. We've been looking for the twenty-first section, or a pledge by the twenty-first section. And there is no twenty-first section."

Rian was staring at her like she was mad, and Tania knew she wasn't doing anything to dissuade the idea. "We couldn't find one," he agreed. "We thought it might have been deleted...?"

"There isn't one. There never was. That *is* the pledge. 'The twenty-first section.' *Those* are the words that activate the mate spell."

Rian froze. "Fask and Leinani just need to say, 'I pledge of the twenty-first section?' That's all?"

Together, they spoke at once, "Speak, *friend,* and enter," and then burst into laughter.

"The words don't have to make sense, there doesn't

have to actually *be* a section twenty-one. It's been right there in front of us this entire time," Rian said in wonder. "You clever, beautiful, amazing queen, you."

But maybe, now, she wouldn't have to be a queen...

The stairs were not the best place for kissing, given Tania's uncertain balance, but she knew that she could never be safer than in Rian's strong arms and when his mouth covered hers, she felt like she'd found her anchor.

27

*T*ania had her head near Raval's and they were poring over the spells spread out over the informal dining room table.

"This is absurd," Raval said crossly. "One of these spells looks like it's to brush *teeth*."

"One of the spells did make one of Rian's leather chairs sprout plush lavender fur," Tania reminded him. "Clearly absurd is not out of the realm of possibility. I don't think this one is even in English. But the handwriting is so terrible, I can't tell."

Rian looked over her far shoulder. "It's not Russian," he said, unhelpfully.

"Is it upside down?" Tania wondered, rotating the page.

"Does *alto* end every one of them?" Raval asked himself.

"If I was going to *hire* someone to make spells for me, I'd want a sure way to turn them all off," Rian suggested.

"Oh good," Fask said, entering with authority, Captain

Luke at his heels. They both looked grim-faced. "You're all here, let's get started."

"Did you get anything out of the prisoner?" Rian wanted to know, taking the seat beside Tania as his brothers and Carina settled into their own chairs. Drayger had clearly not been invited but Rian did not doubt that Luke had already quizzed him thoroughly.

"Some generalized ranting about Small Kingdoms stealing magic from the world," Fask reported. "Nothing useful or specific. He wouldn't tell us anything about Amara or where he was from."

"We *have* traced the missing ice bucket," Captain Luke said. "Not to Majorca, but to Crete."

"Crete?" Toren echoed.

"An island off of Greece," Fask said.

Toren flushed. "I knew *that*. But it's not Small Kingdoms."

"We're starting to think this isn't a matter of a Kingdom rivalry," Fask explained. "He has a tattoo, a black, two-headed axe in the center of a labyrinth. We've tracked the image to a cult that appears to be active in a number of Outside countries."

Tania had picked up one of the pages. "This could be Greek?"

Raval nodded slowly. "Maybe. I still don't think these are all by the same person."

Tania agreed, "I think you're right. These two, I think they could be by the same person." She picked up one of the other spells. "But I'm not sure what either of them *does*. This might be a copy of the spell that froze Rian. It's in Spanish, but I don't know all of these words."

"Got to wonder how many portal spells they have," Tray said, rolling up his placemat and quizzing each of the brothers through it in turn. "They're certainly burning through them trying to get to the Compact."

"Or to Tania," Rian reminded him.

"Tania wasn't in the vault," Toren observed.

Tray grinned. "Or in her room…"

Rian kicked him under the table and watched Tania's eartips turn red.

"It must have been quite a blow to them," Raval said, not paying them any attention. "Losing all these spells. This is months' worth of work, if not years, altogether."

"Why would anyone spend months on a spell that turns a chair into a muppet?" Tania wanted to know.

"I'd like you to work with Raval and the Caster of the guard to try to figure that out," Fask said to Tania very specifically. "The more we know, the more we can anticipate this new enemy."

"I'd be happy to," Tania agreed.

Rian opened his mouth to protest his exclusion, but Fask fixed him with a steely stare. "I want to go over exactly what you think the Compact wants out of that section twenty-one pledge you figured out."

"Am I off the hook?" Toren asked hopefully.

"We don't know yet," Fask said. Then he looked uncharacteristically uncertain and admitted, "But I've been talking to Leinani and she's agreed to come here and…ah…be my mate, since you two figured out how to make it work."

The entire table stared at him. Carina made a little delighted squeal and clapped her hands.

Fask continued, "The king and queen of Mo'oera have given their blessing, and all parties grant that a marriage of convenience would be beneficial for everyone. They've already gone through the motions required and she'll be here next week for Toren and Carina's wedding."

"Well, there's finally a crown princess you won't have to give deportment lessons to and teach to dance," Carina laughed, winking across the table to Tania.

"They wouldn't really have tried to get me to dance, would they?" Tania laughed in return as the others chattered in speculation.

Rian was not sure he had ever seen Fask look this particular combination of embarrassed and yearning. He, of all of them, was always serious and driven and it was odd to see him looking so vulnerable. Rian found himself gazing at Tania's profile as she smiled across the table at Carina.

Fask should be so lucky, he thought achingly. Finding his mate had completed him in ways that he'd never even imagined was possible. She was his other half, his perfect match. Destiny, good luck, things that Rian hadn't even thought to put stock in. He was so glad that he'd been led to her, and he loved her so completely.

Fask got control of himself quickly and frowned down the table to put a stop to the nattering that has risen up in the wake of his news. "We still have a wedding to finish planning," he reminded them. "And enemies to track down; I don't think they are done with us yet. Captain Luke has new security measures to discuss; I give the room to her."

Captain Luke stood and swiftly ran them all through new protective restrictions while Rian shamelessly daydreamed about Tania. Would she marry him, now that there was less chance of being queen? He could just imagine a quiet little ceremony in the receiving rooms; she'd be in one of those white filmy, floaty things, with eyes only for him, and he'd carry her the whole length of the aisle at the end and skip the reception to take her immediately back to his rooms—her rooms, if his were still under reconstruction.

He'd wait a few days before he asked again, he decided, give the dust a little time to settle, try not to look too *desperate*.

"Is that alright with you, Rian?" Fask asked into his pleasant plans.

"Sure," Rian said, having no idea what he'd agreed to. Hopefully Tania had been listening and could fill him in later. She was smiling at him, a shy, warm smile just for him. "*Whatever.*"

Fask didn't look particularly convinced, but apparently the meeting was concluded and Raval started collecting up the spell sheets as everyone pushed back their chairs.

Rian caught Tania's cane as it slipped off the edge of her chair and offered his hand to help her stand. She accepted it, and, to his delight, left her hand in his as they left the dining room. Instead of turning towards the living wing, she tugged him out to gaze out the broad windows of the second floor receiving rooms.

The sun was in its prolonged descent through snow-covered forest. The entire sky was golden-orange, with puffy magenta clouds; they were fast approaching the time of year when lengthy sunrise ran straight to dreamy sunset, with little real daylight between.

"I can't get over how beautiful it is here," she sighed, leaning comfortably into him. "I don't know why I expected it to be drab and gray. Coming to Alaska in winter seemed like the stupidest thing I could do."

"I'm glad you like it here," Rian said sincerely. "I can't wait to show it to you in the summer." Then doubt hit him. She hadn't said yes to forever; would she even still be here in the summer? It seemed impossible to imagine his life without her anymore.

"I guess Fask will be announcing his engagement at Toren and Carina's wedding," Tania said with a sigh.

"We'll be freeeee!" Rian tried to tease.

"For certain definitions of freedom that don't include 'freedom is slavery' from *1984*," Tania said quietly. "Anyway, I had...gotten used to the idea that we were going to announce our engagement then. I guess we'll have to pick a different time."

It took a moment for Rian to understand the meaning of what she was saying, and he jerked his gaze from the sunset to stare at her. "You mean...?"

She looked up at him shyly. "If it's still on the table. I mean, we'll probably have to invite my mother to the wedding, and I come with...other baggage..."

Rian bent to gather her into his arms, and then remembered that he was supposed to be on one knee for the actual request. "Marry me," he begged, sinking before her onto both of them. "Marry me and be my everything."

"How can I be your everything if you're my everything? Doesn't that create some kind of causal loop?" Tania asked, eyes sparkling. When she bent to put her lips to his, Rian pulled her gently down with him and kissed her until they were both out of breath.

"I was afraid you'd think I only agreed to marry you because Fask was going to be king," she confessed, when he finally released her mouth. "But I have wanted to say yes for so long now..." She smiled at him. "I love you, Rian. I would be a queen for you, if I had to."

Rian made a low noise in his throat. "I would be king for you," he told her in return. "I would be *anything* for you, I would *do* anything. I love you, *t.perez*, my fairy queen."

She smiled almost tearfully in return. "*Northernbookwyrm*," she giggled. "I love you, my dragon prince."

Rian had to kiss her again, and again, and then he wasn't waiting for a ceremony, quiet or otherwise, to pick her up and carry her back to her rooms to claim her completely.

EPILOGUE

The hot springs were far more crowded and frenetic than the last time Tania had been there.

The resort, already a luxury winter wonderland, was decorated and fancied up to a whole new level, and there were servants, craftsmen, press, and servers rushing around in near-panic as they readied for visiting royalty.

Fask was adorably nervous about meeting his bride-to-be, and he paced and roared orders and asked Mrs. James about the visitor arrival schedules so often that Tania had them memorized the first day.

Captain Luke was so tightly wound that Tania thought that she might actually witness a spontaneous combustion. Mrs. James wrung her hands and juggled schedules and rosters so complicated that Tania wasn't even sure how she managed to keep them straight.

Of all of them, Tania thought that Carina and Toren, as bride and groom, were actually the least nervous. Toren had shaved off his nascent mustache, with a lot of sighing and complaining, and he and Carina had been fitted for complete wardrobes—not just for the ceremony, but for the pre-ceremony and the reception, and a series of photographs afterwards. They even had special wedding bathing suits for a soak after the ceremony.

The two were light-hearted about the whole thing, and spent most of their time trying to stay out of the way.

"Oh my God," Carina said, shutting the door behind her as she came to hide in Tania's room. "You are so lucky that all you have to do is hold flowers."

"You don't want me trying to walk down the aisle," Tania pointed out as she put her book down. "It was lovely of you to ask me to be your bridesmaid, though."

"Are you sure you aren't going to announce your engagement yet? It's not like the gossip magazines aren't going to guess. Look at that rock!" Carina lifted Tania's hand, glittering with a ring that she still hadn't gotten used to wearing.

"I don't want to steal any of Fask's thunder," Tania said demurely. "That's the marriage that really *matters*."

Carina gave an exaggerated sigh of relief. "I am so, so grateful. It's like a death row pardon."

"Tell me about it," Tania agreed, and they shared a warm smile.

There was a knock on the door. "Come in," Carina called. Then she looked at Tania and covered her mouth in embarrassment. "Sorry, this is your room."

"No worries, Your *Highness*," Tania teased her.

Carina made a noise of despair. "Never call me that again."

Rian tentatively opened the door, looking prepared to duck immediately back out. "You confused me, Carina."

"We've switched places," Carina said, straight-faced but dancing-eyed. "I talked Tania into marrying Toren instead. You get to marry *me* tomorrow."

Rian played along with twice the deadpan as he settled

in the chair next to Tania. "What do you use for bookmarks in your books?" he asked solemnly.

Carina looked confused. "Uh, whatever? Usually I bend a corner."

Tania and Rian both made noises of dismay and despair.

"Sorry, Carina, I can't marry you," Rian said. "I'd have to kill you for that transgression. and there is very specific language in the Compact about murder."

There was another knock at the door. "Come in!" Tania called this time.

"Can I hide here?" Toren asked plaintively. "Oh, Carina! I'm not hiding from *you*!"

"Sure, sure," Carina said, sliding to the side of the couch so he could sit beside her. "Likely story."

Tania just caught the edge of a significant look between Toren and Rian. "There's a delivery for you," Toren said with too much innocence. "They're holding it at the event hall."

Rian was too bland-faced to be for real and Tania knew he had something up his sleeve, no matter how casually he said, "I guess I'll go see what it is." He barely brushed a hand over her shoulders as he left, and Tania reminded herself that she couldn't feel his excitement; she was only guessing at it from the swiftness of his step.

She barely had time to squint suspiciously at Toren, who was clearly in on something, before there was another knock on the door.

This time, both women called out in chorus, "Come *in*!"

Tray opened the door looking like he'd just stuck his hand in an electrical socket. "Rian," he said breathlessly. "*Rian.?*"

"Complete sentences are nice," Toren told him. "You

should try them sometime. Rian's just hopped to the event hall to pick up a delivery." He frowned in concern. "Are you...alright?"

Tray took two long strides into the room, came to a complete stop, and said, "Yes. No. It's a disaster."

"What?" Carina demanded. "What's a disaster?"

"Everything!" Tray said, wild-eyed and sounding desperate. Then he fled the room as abruptly as he'd come.

"What's a disaster?!" Carina demanded after him. "Dammit, it's my wedding, what have you done?" She got to her feet. "Come on Toren, we've got a wedding to save. *Our* wedding!"

"Are you sure we can't run away?" Toren begged, following her to the door.

"Sorry, love," Carina said, laughing at him. "They've already reserved us seventeen pages in Crown Magazine."

Rian was edging in the door as they left, a long, narrow box in his arms. "Do I want to know?" he asked as they went laughing down the hallway and he shut the door.

"Tray was here looking for you," Tania told him, eyeing the box curiously. "He looked...unsettled."

"Tray hates these formal things," Rian said with a shrug. "He's even worse than Toren at being diplomatic."

"Promise me that we can have a nice, quiet wedding," Tania begged.

"I promise that we won't have seventeen pages in Crown Magazine," Rian said, rolling his eyes.

"What's in the box?" Tania could not resist asking any longer.

Rian grinned. "It's for you."

"I guessed," Tania said. "And I'm pretty sure it's not a book."

It was a long box, long enough that she had to stretch

her arms out to take it from him. It was fairly heavy, and she balanced it in her lap and lifted up the top.

"I wasn't sure if they'd have it finished in time for the wedding," Rian said nervously, hovering over her. "But apparently being a prince of Alaska really does get you extra swift service."

"It's a cane!" Tania said in awe. "Oh my gosh, I've never seen one so pretty."

"Try it!" Rian begged. "I've been watching how you use yours, and I asked them to make it just a little heavier, with just a little more hook to the handle in case you need to do battle with it again. Does it fit your hand? Is it right? Do you *like* it?"

Tania felt tears stinging at her eyes. She put the rubber-tipped end of it carefully down on the floor, marveling at the stained wood carving all along the length. It was absolutely nothing like her ugly, insurance-grade cane. It had a fanciful, romantic design, with delicate spirals and inset semi-precious stones that seemed to glow.

It was the perfect cane for a fairy queen and when she stood up and leaned on it carefully, it was exactly the right height. She took a tentative step, and then another. It was a little heavier than her previous cane, and she liked the extra heft. She experimented with her hand position; the handle was delightfully lumpy and there were several ways to hold it. She took some more experimental steps, and marched across the room and back

Rian, as far as she could tell, had not taken a single breath since she'd stood.

"I love it!" she declared and his face fell into a grin of relief.

"I'm so glad," he said. "I wanted it to be perfect."

"You are," Tania said, blinking back happy tears. "You are perfect."

"There's more in the box," Rian said, almost shyly.

Tania used her amazing new cane to return to the couch where she'd left it, diving into the tissue paper with her free hand.

All she came up with were— "Oh, I think you left the receipts in here. You probably don't want me to see these."

"Those aren't receipts for *your* cane," Rian said leadingly.

Tania looked closer at the pages. "Five *hundred* hand-carved canes?"

"They aren't as fancy as yours," Rian said swiftly. "That's one-of-a-kind. But you said that no one should have to make do with the ugly ones that insurance covers. This won't be enough for everyone of course, but the workshop said they couldn't make more than that in three months, so we're starting here. They'll be distributed to all the clinics and village health centers."

Tania made herself close her mouth as soon as she realized that it was hanging open, and she flipped to the next receipt, only to find herself opening it again in astonishment. "This is so much!"

"You shouldn't have to be royalty to get decent medical care," Rian told her firmly, and Tania recognized her own words. "This ought to go a little ways and help a few people, at least. I've hired an advisor to make sure that it goes to the people who need it, and that the application process isn't a nightmare and that there aren't any weird tax loopholes, and even though it's all been done in your name, you don't have to make a single speech or attend any receptions."

Tania was glad of her new cane then, because she felt so many things that she wasn't sure of her balance. "Oh, Rian," she said weakly.

"Was it too much?" Rian asked in concern. "Over the

top? Should I have asked first? Am I an ass for making a gift around a disability?"

"I pray thee, gentle mortal, sing again..."

"My fairy queen," he said in delight, and then Tania was weeping into his shoulder with happy abandon as he scooped her into his arms.

"It is the nicest thing anyone has ever done in the history of the world," she said sincerely. "I am delighted with it. There's just one thing..."

"Anything," Rian promised.

"You have to tell me what the bet was that made you walk around the palace naked for a week!"

Rian's face transformed into an unexpected expression of delight and mischief. "Anything but *that!*"

Tania, laughing, tried to tickle him, but was too pinned in his arms. "I'm dying of curiosity," she complained. "How can I be married to you and not know that story?"

"I'll show you how," Rian promised, and then he was kissing her, her neck and her ear, his clever hands finding all the places of her body that he knew so well.

By the time he'd gotten her dress unbuttoned, she had forgotten her prying altogether, and the only nude Rian she cared about was the one who could be with her, here and now, and who completed her entirely.

A NOTE FROM ELVA BIRCH

Thank you so much for reading my book! I had a wonderful time writing about Tania and Rian, and I can't wait to dig in on the next book...read to the end for a sneak preview!

Your reviews are very much appreciated; I read them all and they help other readers decide whether or not to buy my books! A huge thank you to all of my fabulous beta readers and copy editors; any errors that remain are entirely my own. If you find typos — or you'd just like share your thoughts with me! — please feel free to email me at elvaherself@elvabirch.com. My cover was designed by Ellen Million.

To find out about my new releases, you can follow me on Amazon, subscribe to my newsletter, or like me on Facebook. Join my Reader's Retreat on Facebook for sneak previews and cut scenes. Find all the links at my webpage: elvabirch.com

I also write under other pen names—keep reading for information about my other available titles...

MORE BY ELVA BIRCH

A Day Care for Shifters: A hot new full-length series about adorable shifter kids and their struggling single parents in a town full of mystery and surprise. Start the series with Wolf's Instinct, when Addison comes to Nickel City to take a job at a very special day care and finds a family to belong to. A gentle ice-cream-straight-from-the-container escape. Sweet and sizzling!

~

The Royal Dragons of Alaska: A fascinating alternate world where Alaska is ruled by secret dragon shifters. Adventure, romance, and humor! Reluctant royalty, relentless enemies…dogs, camping, and magic! Start with The Dragon Prince of Alaska.

~

Suddenly Shifters: A hilarious series of novellas, serials, and shorts set in the small town of Anders Canyon, where something (in the water?) is making ordinary citizens turn into shifters. Start with Something in the Water! Also available in audio!

~

Birch Hearts: An enchanting collection of short stories and novellas. Unconstrained by theme or setting, each short read has romance, magic, and heart, with a satisfying conclusion. And always, the impossible and irresistible. Start with a sampler plate in Prompted 2 for fourteen pieces of sweet-to-sizzling flash fiction, or dive in with the novella, Better Half. Breakup is a free story!

WRITING AS ZOE CHANT

Shifting Sands Resort: A complete ten-book series - plus two collections of shorts. This is a thrilling shifter romance set at a tropical island resort. Each book stands alone but connects into a great mystery with a thrilling conclusion. Start with Tropical Tiger Spy or dive in to the Omnibus edition, with all of the novels, short stories, and novellas in my preferred reading order!

~

Fae Shifter Knights: A complete four-book fantasy portal romp, with cute pets and swoon-worthy knights stuck in a world of wonders like refrigerators and ham sandwiches. Start with Dragon of Glass!

~

Green Valley Shifters: A sweet, small town series with single dads, secret shifters, sweet kids, and spinsters. Lowperil and steamy! Standalone books where you can revisit your favorite characters - this series is also complete! Start with Dancing Barefoot! Green Valley Shifters crosses over with **Virtue Shifters**. Start with Timber Wolf!

THE BOOK I'M NOT WRITING

Writing as Elva Birch
She's got one life to live

Anita takes a chance at a job she's not sure she can handle and she's tickled pink when the gorgeous billionaire picks her little bakery to cater his big charity event. But what was supposed to be the opportunity of a lifetime turns into the storm of a century.

He's got one leg to stand on

Frank Wilson has built his reputation and his world-spanning lawn ornament business on one tenet: honesty. There's nothing fake about Frank Wilson -- not his fabulous fortune or his amazing physique.

...or his inner flamingo.

Trapped together with his fated mate in his big empty office building with two thousand gourmet cupcakes and no power, Frank is sure that -- finally -- nothing will stand between him and everything that he'd ever wanted, in the arms of a curvy woman wearing an apron. The only problem is, she's not interested in settling down to join his flock.

And to win her heart, he's going to have to put his foot down.

～

I love to do harmless April Fool's Day pranks, and I made this cover for my readers, even going so far as to make a book blurb and fake Amazon book preview image for Facebook.

But the joke's on me and this, of all of the books I have planned, is the one I have the most readers clamoring for!

I am not writing it. I am not writing the scene where Anita plays Simon Says and makes Frank stand on one foot forever. I am not plotting the chapter where they are dancing around the empty ballroom. I am not researching all the flamingo jokes on the internet.

If you would like to read more of the book I'm very definitely not writing, you'll have to sign up for my mailing list at elvabirch.com or join Elva Birch's Readers Retreat at Facebook!

SNEAK PREVIEW OF THE DRAGON PRINCE'S BRIDE

"Yes, Mother," Leinani said.

She wasn't actually sure what she was replying to; all of her attention was outside the window, at the snowy landscape flying by outside their car. But 'Yes, Mother,' was a safe reply to just about anything.

She wished they were going slower, there was so much to see, and it made her dizzy to watch the strange trees dash by.

And, to be honest, she was in no hurry to arrive at their destination.

It was so surreal, to be in an arranged marriage, in this day and age. Leinani hadn't really expected to marry for love, but she'd thought that maybe she wouldn't have to marry at all.

She'd pictured a life of supporting her parents, of watching her brothers marry, of hiking Belvedere Lookout and flying down to the beach in the sea-scented air, catching updrafts and swimming in the reef-sheltered bays.

And if she *had* thought to anticipate marriage, it would

not have been to Fask, the oldest prince of Alaska, in order to cement an alliance that already felt secure.

But Mo'orea honored loyalty, and Alaska needed a queen for their eldest son, so here she was, thousands of miles north of her home, hurrying to bind herself to a complete stranger with a magical spell.

Fask had been kind, in their correspondence, and their conversations on the phone had been reassuring. They'd found common ground; he had a sense of humor, he was certainly handsome enough and it was all going to work out just fine.

She was going to marry Prince Fask and be Queen of Alaska, and that was just the way it was.

Her mother said something else she didn't catch, and Leinani again said, "Yes, Mother," and hoped it would suffice.

Angel Hot Springs Resort opened out of the forest around them, a busy little cluster of buildings milling with people. Guards at the front gate waved them through.

Leinani took a deep breath and soothed her fluttering nerves.

Soon.

There would be a lengthy ceremony for Toren and Carina's marriage, and then a quiet, private activation of the mate bond according to the Compact...and then...

She scratched a little hole in the frost gathering on the window as the car slowly approached the largest building, with its impressively tall double doors. She could probably enter it in her dragon form.

Here, her dragon said, rising suddenly within her. *We are supposed to be here, **now.***

It was so undeniable, utterly irresistible. Leinani felt a wave of relief crash over her. It felt like everything was happening exactly as it should, and she was, for the first time, completely *comfortable* with the destiny that had been chosen for her. She was going to meet her mate, and they would marry, and she would be a queen, just as she was meant to be.

She slipped from the car as soon as it rolled to a stop, smiling at the uniformed guard who took her hand to help her out. The guard was a Native woman with chin tattoos and golden buttons who didn't smile back.

It didn't dampen Leinani's relief in the slightest, and she moved forward confidently, not even waiting for her parents behind her. The air was bitingly cold, but the bitter temperature didn't bother her; it was something else entirely that had Leniani stepping forward as swiftly as she could for the waiting hall.

There, her dragon breathed in her head, leading her unerringly up the steps. Guards saluted as she passed them and opened one of the double doors before her.

It was warm inside, and mist swirled with her into the bright-lit lobby.

Had they already performed the ceremony? It wasn't the plan, and she hadn't thought that was possible without her participation, but the draw was absolutely unmistakable. She shrugged out her coat and let them lift it from her, then marched, not through the double doors into the hall where the guests were milling in anticipation of the start of the wedding itself, but to a smaller door through a hallway on the left.

No one thought to stop her.

Leinani didn't pause, didn't hesitate even a moment. She turned to a narrow stairway tucked behind a corner, gathered her tapa cloth skirt into her hands, and was halfway up when a figure appeared at the top, hurrying towards her with the exact same urgency.

They stopped just a step apart, and Leinani, already at

a disadvantage due to her diminutive height, had to crane her head awkwardly back to look up at...*him.*

It was Fask, the oldest prince of Alaska. Her husband-to-be.

She was confident that he would make her happier than she'd ever had any reason to hope she could be, and Leinani couldn't *wait* to make him her own.

There was winter sunlight streaming in through a window to their right, and his dark hair was aglow in gold, his face shadowed as he stared down at her.

Leinani felt giddy, awash with eagerness and delight. Her dragon felt incandescent in her chest, happy and confident and slightly smug, the way she often was.

Then he very suddenly sat down, so hard that the stairs trembled, and they were gazing at each other, face to face.

Leinani's heart dropped from her chest and dismay quenched her desire.

This was unmistakably her mate, but it wasn't *Fask* at all.

Preorder The Dragon Prince's Bride now!

The Dragon Prince's Bride will be available in 2021!

Printed in Dunstable, United Kingdom